Secret Obsessions

Secret Temptations, Volume 1

Cameron Hart

Published by Cameron Hart, 2024.

SECRET OBSESSIONS

First edition. June 27, 2024.

ISBN: 979-8227919328

Written by Cameron Hart.

Want a free book?

Sign up for my newsletter[1] and get your free copy of Chasing Stacy!

One look at the stunning waitress carrying the weight of the world on her shoulders, and I'm a goner. I wasn't looking for a sweet little thing with auburn hair and more baggage than I can fit on the back of my bike, but there's no going back now. She's mine. I'll prove to her I'm more than capable of handling her past and making her feel safe again.

---

1. https://dl.bookfunnel.com/7wbqvhsx8r

Chapter One

Dylan

I take a look around the lecture hall, frowning when I see just how big it is. How many students are registered for this class? As the professor, I should probably know. It's been ages since I've taught underclassmen, however, let alone an intro course.

Digging around in my satchel, I grab my laptop and navigate to the university's teacher portal to check the class roster for *Philosophy 101*. One hundred and twenty five students. That can't be right. I knew these lectures were large, but I had no idea I'd be dealing with so many snot-nosed freshmen all at once.

"Fuck," I mutter to myself. The word echoes around the empty room, and I rub the back of my neck, trying to massage away the migraine creeping up on me.

The podium is on the ground level, giving me a good look at the four platforms of desks surrounding me in a semicircle. Soon, the chairs will be filled, and this horrible class will begin. I can hardly wait.

Ironically, teaching is my least favorite part of this gig. As a tenured professor of philosophy, I rarely interact with anyone who isn't a colleague or a doctoral student. It's been damn near a decade since I've had to deal with underclassman, and I've cherished every minute.

My days are usually spent overseeing field studies, writing articles for respected, peer-reviewed journals, and generally making the university look good for having me on their payroll. Hey, it's not bragging if it's true.

I check my Rolex, noting that class starts in fifteen minutes. I mutter to myself as I gather the syllabus from my briefcase, making sure the pages are stapled correctly. Smirking, I look over the thick packet of paper. These students have no idea what they're getting themselves into. This may be a 101 class, but I'm not a 101 professor. They'll be working hard to earn their grades.

I've loved my job and career thus far, and God knows I've fought hard to get to where I'm at today. What started out as an escape from my dreadful childhood blossomed into a passion for knowledge. I remember sneaking off into an empty field on the ranch with any and every book I could find. Sometimes I'd stay there for hours, until I was certain my father had moved on from an alcohol-induced rage to sleeping on the couch.

When I got older, I became enamored with not only *what* we know, but *how* we know it. That's when I stumbled upon epistemology, a branch of philosophy that studies the origin of knowledge and how we got to where we are today.

The soft click of the door at the back of the room pulls me from my thoughts. A skinny kid with a backwards hat and jeans that are far too tight comes stumbling in, followed by a few more early bird students.

I keep my head down, not wanting to acknowledge them just yet. I have to remind myself that I'm doing this for a friend. It's not charity work, technically, but it sure feels that way.

I'm usually surrounded by people who are motivated to learn more, push harder, and think about the world abstractly. This semester, however, I've traded that in for several intro classes filled with hormonal teenagers who only think with one part of their bodies. Hint, it's not their brains.

However, when the dean, Reed Landis, called me up last week, I had no choice. Reed is my closest friend. My only friend, if I'm honest, but that's not important. I don't understand people on the whole. They confuse and irritate me. Reed has stuck by me for far longer than the time we've worked together, though.

We grew up in the same shitty town in South Dakota. Reed knows better than anyone the difficulties of living with an alcoholic caregiver. His dad was always in and out of their lives, leaving Reed and his two sisters, Christy, and Emmaline, in the hands of their mother. She drowned her sorrows in bottle after bottle of vodka, leaving her children to run wild and fend for themselves.

All that to say, Reed and I have history, and when he asks me for a favor, I'm sure as hell going to follow through. Even if it sucks.

My best friend got the terrible news that his sister, Christy, and her husband were in a fatal car accident a few weeks ago. They left behind a six-year-old daughter, who is now in Reed's custody. The poor guy is not only wading through shock and grief, but now the perma-bachelor has to figure out how to take care of a little girl.

Emmaline offered to help, but she's much younger, just starting out life on her own in a new state, away from her awful parents. Reed certainly has the means to take care of a kid, just not the disposition.

On top of all of that, Christy worked for the university, teaching freshman philosophy courses. That's where I come in. I can't help Reed with the kid, but I can pick up Christy's classes so it's one less thing for my friend to worry about.

With a renewed sense of purpose, I check my watch again, seeing it's one minute until go time. Looking up, I note the room has filled up with chattering students. There's the usual spread of jocks in sweatpants and jerseys and girls wearing short shorts and crop tops to try and impress said jocks. I also observe which students are hungover on the first day of class, making a note next to their names on my roster. Almost everyone has their phone out, some taking selfies while others type away furiously, most likely on social media or dating apps.

God, I already hate every single one of them, but I need to suck it up.

While the lecture hall is pretty full, I know a few students are still missing. They have exactly thirty-five seconds to get their ass in their seats before I mark them tardy on the first day.

If there's one thing I can't stand, it's tardiness. Scanning over the list of student names, my eyes catch on one miss Sarah Robbins. The senator's daughter. *Great.* Reed mentioned that Senator Robbins' daughter was added to the roster last-minute as a favor. She's in her senior year, but probably spent her college career partying instead of studying, which is why she has to make up credits with a freshman course.

"This is *Philosophy 101*," I announce, my deep voice projecting into the large room and causing every eye to snap in my direction. "If you're not supposed to be here, then take the next ten seconds to get the hell out."

A few students dart their eyes down to their desks, while others shift uncomfortably in their seats. Good. They need to know I'm not going to take any of their bullshit.

Some might say I'm strict or even cruel at times, but that's not the case. At least, it's not my intention. I just don't have the kind of disposition to sugar coat anything. Why waste my breath and time with pleasantries when at the end of the day, every conversation is merely an exchange of information? It's not rude, it's efficient.

My gaze sweeps the room, almost in challenge. Go ahead, freshmen. Admit you got lost on your first day of class. I dare you.

One brave student slips out of his chair and grabs his backpack, scrambling toward the exit. Another one follows, then three more. The last kid nearly trips up the steps to get to the back door, and I barely suppress a grin. I'll admit, it's kind of fun to scare freshmen. That's the only upside to this gig.

"Good. Now that we have that settled–"

I'm interrupted by the door swinging open and banging against the wall. A low growl scrapes my throat as my migraine pushes to the surface. Being interrupted is right next to tardiness on my list of grave annoyances. This day is getting better and better.

I'm about to tell whoever is walking in late to turn around and book it, but then I get a good look at her.

Standing there, at the back of the lecture hall, is the most enchanting creature I've ever seen. The universe skips a beat, pausing for a infinitesimally small moment to let me soak up everything about her.

The light from the hallway illuminates her curves, silhouetting her mouthwatering body as she takes a tentative step forward. I want to memorize the way her body moves. My eyes latch onto her rounded hips, swaying back and forth, back and forth, as she walks down the aisle to look for a seat.

She's in leggings and an oversized, off-the-shoulder sweater. It's nothing overtly sexy, yet all I want to do is rip that damn shirt off of her and see what's concealed beneath it. There's no mistaking her large breasts pulling against the fabric, or her thick thighs as they rub together with each step. Christ, I want to touch her there, spread her thighs open so I can have a good look at her hidden little treasure. Fuck, I need to study every inch of her soft skin, taking note of what makes her shiver, what makes her moan, what makes her cry out my name as she drowns in ecstasy.

I watch, completely dumbfounded, as she makes her way to a desk and sits down. Her midnight black hair is swept off to one side, the long tendrils hanging over her shoulder, while bright, clear eyes blink back at me. Holy hell, what color is that? Ice blue mixed with teal and something else. Something mysterious and addictive. I've never had an inappropriate thought about a student before. I don't like it. That's not who I am, though I've gotten plenty of offers over the years.

My gaze wanders down her face, taking in her dainty nose, rounded cheeks, and soft, full lips. I have the sudden urge to taste those lips, suck on one and then the other, teasing this sexy vixen to the point of madness before giving into the ultimate pleasure.

Instead, I push all thoughts of fucking my student out of my head, and berate her for being late.

"Tardiness is not tolerated in my class, Miss…?"

The woman inhales sharply, her eyes growing impossibly wider. "Robbins," she replies. "Sarah Robbins."

"Of course," I mutter. The senator's daughter. That information lands like a brick to the stomach. It should eviscerate any lustful thoughts I have, and I'm sure it will. Soon. Very soon.

"What was that?" she questions, surprising the hell out of me.

"I said, tardiness is unacceptable. You've now started the semester with one late mark on your record. I have a three-strike system, so don't make a habit of showing up late."

I'm about to hand out the syllabus when little miss tardy speaks up. "To be fair, the room number for this course is wrong. My official schedule from the registrar says this class is in room *two* fifty, not *one* fifty."

I grunt, not liking her tone. Or maybe liking it too much.

"Everyone else seemed to have figured it out, Miss Robbins." I turn my attention back to the task at hand, but the annoying woman speaks again.

"For someone who has made a career out of the study of knowledge, I'd think you would make sure the information disseminated to your students was accurate." A few snickers echo around the room as I turn my full attention to Sarah fucking Robbins.

Who does she think she is to call me out like this? On the first day of class? More importantly, why is my dick harder than it's been in years? I gave up on relationships over a decade ago, after my last girlfriend told me my attention and passion were suffocating her. Haven't slept with anyone since. What's the point? Right now, however, my body is letting me know it's been too long going without. Not that I'll be finding relief with my student, for fuck's sake. That would be insane. Career suicide. Not gonna happen.

I open my mouth to scold her, but end up swallowing my tongue when Sarah levels a challenging stare at me. Her teal blue eyes sparkle with the barest hint of a challenge, like she's enjoying this interaction.

While the look tears the breath from my lungs, I can't give her the upper hand on day one. Or ever. Yes, I better shut this shit down before... well, it's just best to squash whatever this is.

"Don't expect to get a free ride just because your father is a senator, Miss Robbins. This will be a difficult course, and I have neither the time nor the patience to coddle spoiled princesses."

Those expressive eyes of hers dim slightly, and her shoulders drop. I can see her shut down, sinking into herself as she holds her notebook in front of her like a shield.

Good. Mission accomplished.

Then why do I feel like a total asshole?

Chapter Two

Sarah

As soon as Professor Cole dismisses us, I throw everything in my backpack and run out of the classroom, though I can't seem to escape the effect of his gaze.

The second I stepped into the classroom, his golden brown eyes pinned me into place. I felt his gaze everywhere as it wandered up and down my body, though surely I was imagining that. My father never fails to remind me of my curves and how I could stand to lose a few pounds if I ever want to catch a husband.

I shake those thoughts in my head as a rush out of the building, chasing down a bus right before it leaves the stop. I grin as I step inside, knowing my father hates when I use public transportation. It's unbecoming for someone of my stature, according to him. Whatever the hell that means.

I plop down on the first available seat, huffing and puffing and out of breath, though I'm not sure if it's from my rush to get here or the lingering effects of Professor Cole. I knew he was a big deal in the university - after all, my father did request me to take his class, specifically. All the best for me right?

I roll my eyes, knowing my father never has my best interest at heart. He resents the fact that he's paying for my education as a nurse, but we have an agreement. As long as I show up whenever, wherever he dictates in my best dress, hair up, and makeup painted on, I can finish out my degree. I hate being fake and perpetuating this lie that we're the perfect, all-American family. Truthfully, we're anything but.

It's no secret my father always wanted a son, someone to carry on his name and be truly proud of. He has to make do with me, however. As a lowly female, in his opinion, all I'm good for is marrying off and hopefully marrying up.

Speaking of, my phone buzzes with a reminder that I have another stuffy dinner tonight with my dad and his insufferable circle of friends.

Groaning internally, I mentally go over the dresses I have stuffed to the back of my closet. They aren't my style at all, but that doesn't matter. My father paid a stylist to pick out dresses to highlight my assets and hide my flaws. As a result, I have a wardrobe full of cocktail dresses that reveal far too much of my ample cleavage, and have a corset that squeezes all of my extra weight and somehow shoves it into my ribcage.

Coupled with four-inch heels I've never quite mastered, I always feel like a sausage stuffed in a casing, wobbling around like a baby deer. My father's so-called friends, especially their sons, don't seem to care. Whenever I'm forced to go to these dinners and parties, I want to cover up with a blanket or throw a winter coat on.

I shiver, thinking about the hungry eyes I'll face tonight. They always find my cleavage, my thighs, and really anywhere to look except for my eyes. I hate the way their looks make me feel; gross, on display, and uncomfortable in my own skin. But most of all, I feel cheap.

Professor Cole's gaze, however, was completely different. While it appeared he seemed to look at all the same places, my body responded with a warm tickling heat that I've never experienced before. It started in my belly and slowly slid down toward my center. As soon as I sat down in my seat, I pressed my thighs together to find some relief for the pressure pulsing between them.

But then he opened his mouth.

That's how I know I must've been making everything up between us. Of course I was. I'm never just me. I'm never Sarah Robbins. I'm always the senator's daughter. And that's exactly what Professor Cole saw.

It doesn't matter that I'm well behaved and get good grades. People think they know me because they know my father. They know he's a greedy philanderer who wields his power like a sword, ready to cut down anyone who crosses him.

If people took time to get to know me, they'd see I'm nothing like that. In fact, I'm nothing like the other spoiled rich kids who run in the same socialite circles. While the peers in my income bracket are out partying, sleeping around, and generally being idiots, I've kept my head down.

I was on the debate team in high school for goodness sake. Nothing screams page six scandal like lettering in debate and graduating valedictorian, right? I've never even had a boyfriend, or a kiss for that matter. Basically, I'm the most boring person in existence, but I still get lumped in with the trouble-making trust fund babies. Or, as Professor Cole so gracefully put it, the spoiled princesses.

My stop is announced and I pull the cord above my head, signaling I'd like to get off. Gathering my things, I hop off the bus and scurry to my apartment, looking forward to an hour of solitude before I have to get ready for tonight.

I greet the doorman, Jeff, and give him a warm smile as I head back to the elevators. Most of the other residents treat Jeff like a servant, barely glancing his way when he holds the door for them. I would be surprised if any of them knew his name.

I don't understand how people can be so rude. Jeff is a sweet older gentleman who used to work security before he had back surgery a few years ago. He's been here for five years, and plans to retire at the end of the year. Jeff always thanks me for my kindness, which makes my heart hurt. I'm simply treating him the way everyone should be treated; with dignity and respect. Jeff tells me that's why I'll be such a good nurse. God, I hope so.

The elevator dings, and as soon as the doors open, I step inside and slump against the back wall, heaving out of breath.

Even though I've grown up with wealth my entire life, I'm still not used to the opulence that greets me when the elevator doors open up into my private penthouse. I wanted to live in the dorms and have the normal college experience, but of course that wouldn't look good for a senator's daughter. I stayed at home the first two years, got good grades, and managed to convince my father to let me live on my own. I had hoped for a simple apartment close to campus, maybe with a few roommates. But my dad insisted on this ridiculous private apartment building with a high-rise, and me living at the very top. A princess in her tall tower.

My brow furrows and fists clench at the reminder of what Professor Cole called me. How could he be such a jerk when it was *his* fault I was late! When I pointed that out to him, though, his amber eyes glinted and his jaw tensed. And then he dealt the death blow, calling me a spoiled princess. I mean, what the hell?

I slip my backpack off my shoulders and set it on the breakfast bar as I walk into the kitchen to grab a glass of water. It's crystal of course, not that anyone comes in here and sees my dishes, but that doesn't seem to matter to my father.

Leaning against the sink, I look around the space with gleaming stainless steel appliances, marble countertops, and gorgeous wooden floors that go throughout the entire penthouse. I feel bad that I mostly microwave meals when I have the time to eat at home, but my father didn't ask me what I wanted. Again it's all about appearances.

But I'm so damn tired of being fake.

Honestly, that's a huge reason I wanted to become a nurse. We all wear the same scrubs, we all work long hours, and we're all here to help patients. It's a level playing field. Plus, it's an important job that actually matters. That's really all I want in life. I want to do something meaningful. I want to *be* meaningful. I went to matter to someone.

My phone buzzes, startling me out of my thoughts and back into the moment. I pull my phone out of my backpack and smile when I see my best friend, Faye, is calling me on FaceTime.

Faye also comes from a wealthy family, and like me, she's not into the drama or shallowness that comes with money. Our parents have been friends for longer than we've been alive, so Faye and I have grown up together. I'm so lucky to have someone who understands the pressures of living under a microscope and trying to balance your hopes and dreams with your family's desires.

"Faye, I'm so glad to see your face." Her signature smile lights up the screen and her hazel eyes sparkle. She's a bigger girl like me, but I've always thought she wore her curves better.

"I know, right?" We both laugh as she strikes a pose. Faye is fun, silly, and a firecracker when pushed too far. Basically, she doesn't fit in with her family's idea of a perfect daughter, much like me. That hasn't dimmed her sparkle at all, though. She's kind of my hero.

"How's your mom and her new boyfriend? Do you think this one will stick around?"

"Who knows. I'm surprised she's still with him, honestly. She usually goes for dudes with deep pockets, hefty life-insurance policies, and only a few years to live." Faye rolls her eyes as if it doesn't bother her, but I know my bestie better than that. Her mother clawed her way up into high society the old fashioned way - by being a gold digger. Two ex husbands are still paying her alimony, while the other two are six feet under and still adding to her wealth with their insurance money.

"Maybe she's in love?" I suggest.

Faye stares at me for a moment, and then bursts out laughing. "Good one," she snorts. "I think she likes him because he's a pushover and does her bidding. Unfortunately, that means my mom is looking to me for her next payout."

"What do you mean?" I ask as I wander into my bedroom and flop down on the bed. Faye does the same, flinging herself onto a stack of decorative pillows crowded on her bed.

"It seems I'm joining the ranks of daughters to be wedded off for social status and money."

"Welcome to the club," I say dryly.

"Uh-oh. Another set-up tonight?"

"No, thank God. Just a dinner with the Windgates and Offermans." Faye scrunches up her nose in disgust, then fakes throwing up. I giggle at her antics, knowing all too well how insufferable those two families are. Especially Mr. Windgate. More like Mr. Long Winded. God, his stories last forever, and they aren't interesting or relevant at all. Most of the time, his stories are some backhanded way to put other people down or to humble-brag about his latest ventures.

"Ugh. Let's change the subject before I die of boredom just thinking about them." I readily agree. "How was your first philosophy class?"

I groan and slide my free hand down my face before leveling a look at Faye. "It was horrible. First, the room number was wrong, so I walked into class late. It wasn't even *that* late. Two minutes at most, but that didn't matter to Professor Cole," I mutter.

"OMG, *the* Professor Cole? Is he as rude as everyone says he is?"

"Worse," I confirm with a nod. "He called me out on being late, saying tardiness is unacceptable. For two minutes! On the *first* day!" Faye rolls her eyes, agreeing with me that it's ridiculous. "And to make matters worse, he knew exactly who I was. He said I wouldn't get a free pass and that he didn't have time for spoiled princesses."

"He said that? What the hell, man?" I smile at my bestie's instant loyalty.

"I know," I sigh. "It's going to be a long-ass semester."

"At least it's your last one, right?"

"Yeah. I still can't believe my credits got messed up and I have to take that stupid class." Faye nods sympathetically. She knows all about the fiasco that took place over the summer.

I thought I was all set to graduate, but my advisor looked over my transcripts and realized I was missing a humanity credit. Seriously? At that point, the only class left was philosophy. My advisor tried consoling me by saying all the intro classes were being taught by the renowned Dylan Cole. Too bad he's a total asshole.

Faye's mother shouts something in the background, and my friend jumps before groaning. "Ugh. I gotta go, my mom is in one of her moods."

"It's okay, I should probably go get ready for tonight anyway."

"Good luck!"

"You too."

We hang up and I take one more moment to myself before crawling off the bed and putting on my costume for the night. That's exactly how it feels.

Twenty minutes later, I'm staring at my reflection in the mirror. Red, sequined dress, black heels, and obnoxious diamond chandelier earrings. My father requested that I wear them tonight. Okay, it was more like he demanded, but whatever. The gaudy things are already making my ears hurt, but Dad wants to show off his latest gift, so I don't have a choice.

The ding of an incoming text has me scrambling for my purse - black to match my heels, with a diamond clasp, of course. Pulling out my phone, I see it's my dad.

The car will be there in ten minutes. Make sure to wear your new earrings.

I roll my eyes and text him back before slipping my phone back in my purse. Grabbing a warm shawl, I give my dress a final tug, hoping to cover up more of my chest, but I'm not sure it helped.

By the time I make it out front, a shiny black BMW is waiting for me. Todd, one of several chauffeurs on my family's payroll, opens the car door for me before shutting me inside. The car itself is roomy, but I feel like I'm in a prison cell. We ride off into the night, the sleek vehicle carrying me to the dreaded dinner.

Soon I'll graduate, I tell myself. *Soon I'll be free.*

Chapter Three

Dylan

I watch Miss Robbins chew the end of her pen as she dutifully looks over the test. I can't seem to keep my eyes off of her lips, which appear to be covered in some type of lip gloss, making her that much more irresistible to me.

It's been three weeks of pure torture. I've told myself every Tuesday and Thursday that I'm not going to look at her or give her any attention, that she's not the most captivating woman I've ever seen. Every Tuesday and Thursday I give myself the same peptalk - she's a student, she's too young, she's spoiled, and just plain trouble.

And yet... Here I am, unable to look away. My eyes move on their own, drinking in every inch of her, starting with her sleek black hair. It's up in a messy bun today, showing off her slender neck. Wisps of hair frame her face, and I have to clench my fist to keep myself from tucking them behind her delicate ear. God her skin looks so soft, so pure so... Precious. She's like a damn China doll and I don't know what to do with myself when we're in the same room.

I don't know what to do with myself when we're *not* in the same room either, for that matter. On the days I don't see her, I think about her, and every single night I dream about her. Fuck, my dick lengthens in my dress pants and I shift in my seat, thankful for the heavy desk in between me and my students.

Last night's dream was particularly filthy, the memory still vivid in my mind. I pictured myself sinking into her wet heat, her soft thighs cushioning my hips as rutted into her. Images of my dream come flooding back into my mind, the way her breasts jiggled with each rough thrust, the blush spreading from her cheeks, down her neck, over her chest, and all the way down her stomach, glowing so beautifully for me as we reached our peak together.

It was more than just the feeling of her pussy squeezing my cock that had me coming in my fucking boxers when I woke up; it was her eyes. Light blue with just a hint of green. Her pupils were dilated, the need for release pouring out of her with every touch, every look, every ragged breath. I longed for her pleasure as much as my own. More, even. Jesus, I can't stop thinking about the sounds she would make, the way she'd scream my name as we fall into complete bliss.

The truly fucked up thing is, it's not my first name I long to hear. It's a different title, one I've never gone by before. I've never had fantasies like this, never even thought about it, but now my body can't seem to find peace until I hear the forbidden word drip from her lips. I want to taste it on her tongue, feel her come around me as she moans for more.

More, Daddy. Harder. Please, Daddy...

A student sneezes, ripping me from my taboo thoughts. I blink my eyes a few times trying to clear the graphic memory of the dream. Somehow, I manage to tear my eyes away from Miss Robbins, and glare at the student currently blowing his nose. I know it's not his fault he's sick, or that I'm particularly irritable as of late, but he's going to bear my wrath anyway.

The kid looks up from his Kleenex as if he can sense my annoyance, and quickly puts it away.

I avoid looking at Miss Robbins for all of five seconds before my eyes are drawn back to her curvy figure. She's wearing a gauzy blouse today that's light pink and practically see-through. I could see hints of her white lacy bra peeking through, and I know if I can see it, every other male on campus can see it as well. When she walked in the door, I nearly growled at her to turn back around and change her outfit.

My obsession is getting out of control. I saw her talking to another student outside of the classroom last week, and yelled at the young man to come see me in my office. The guy almost peed his pants as he followed me, and I had to make up some shit excuse to yell at him, but at least I got the fucker away from my girl.

Shit. Not my girl. My *student*. I just have to keep telling myself that.

The worst part is, Miss Robbins isn't just a breathtaking beauty. She's intelligent. Witty. And so fucking sassy. My mouth twitches up into a smirk just thinking about some of her antics over the last few weeks, but I conceal it immediately.

Sarah showed up thirty minutes early to the second day of class. She was already in her seat with her notebook, laptop, and pen out when I walked in. The infuriating woman sat in her seat with her hands folded in her lap and a smug smile on her face during the entire class. I could read her mind as those clear blue eyes followed my every move, her left eyebrow quirked up every once in a while as if in challenge. *I'm here on time, but I'm not learning anything. Promptness doesn't equal a quality education, just like tardiness doesn't equal a bad student.*

I grunt, then attempt to cover up the sound with a cough. Miss Robbins tips her head up, staring right at me before tilting her head to the side in the most adorable way.

"Eyes on your test," I snap, making her jump in her seat.

Sarah rolls her eyes at me and my cock twitches. I'd like to spank her for that little move. I'd bend her over my lap, pull down her leggings, and watch her ass shake with each strike of my hand. Then I'd slip my fingers between her thighs, feeling how wet she is, how much she likes it when I take control. God, I want her to thank me for her punishment, for making her a good girl again.

A snarl claws at my throat as my dick presses against my zipper. I cough again, though it sounds more like a growl. I'm about to lose my goddamn mind right here in the middle of teaching an intro class, all because of one Miss Sarah Robbins.

The curvy angel turns her test over and writes something on the back before standing up and walking toward my desk. I rub a hand over my mouth, scolding myself for watching the way her hips sashay back and forth gracefully with each step.

I'm so lost in her mesmerizing body, I can hardly pull my eyes away when she's finally at my desk, handing me her test. I grab it out of her outstretched hand, careful not to let our fingers touch. I don't trust myself to let her go once I get my hands on her.

"What's this?" I ask harshly, turning the paper over to see her scribbled handwriting. "Note passing is not allowed."

A soft little laugh rings in the air, and I can't help but look up at her. "If I wanted to pass notes in class, I'd just text or get on messenger. Things have changed a bit since your college years." Her blue eyes flash with a wild, excited energy, like going toe to toe with me is a game. Well, I hope she's prepared to lose.

"Indeed. In my day, we earned our education through long study sessions and hard work instead of nepotism."

Miss Robbins shocks the hell out of me when she snorts out a laugh. Her face turns bright red and her small hand comes up to cover her mouth. I stare at her, not sure what to do with her reaction. Isn't she afraid of me? I've been rude, harsh, and demanding ever since I first laid eyes on her. So why is she laughing at me?

"No offense, Professor, but that's bullshit."

My jaw tenses at her flippant tone, and I grit out, "Excuse me?"

"You're telling me that *back in the day*, wealth and social status didn't play a part in higher education. Is that why all of the buildings here on campus have someone's last name on them? Because the university was just so thankful for all of the hard working students and wanted to build libraries in their names?"

Fuck, I can't think when she's talking back to me. The fact that she called me out and made a good counter argument shouldn't have me ready to pull her across this desk and finally claim those tempting lips.

"Isn't *your* last name on the new theater?" I sneer, shoving my confusing feelings to the back of my mind.

Miss Robbins turns from sassy to pissed off in the blink of an eye. Goddamn, I want to kiss that look right off her face and let her work her anger out while riding my dick.

"Believe it or not, I can be a good student and also come from money," she spits out.

"That remains to be seen," I tell her firmly, breaking eye contact with her.

I can feel the frustration coming off of her curvy body in waves. I have no doubt the feisty Miss Robbins wants to punch me square in the jaw, but her upbringing would never allow that. Hitting a tenured professor? Unheard of. And sleeping with one... Shit. I have to stop thinking about that.

Sarah takes the hint, turning on her heel and snatching her backpack off the ground before stomping out the classroom door. Only after I'm sure she's not coming back to give me more of her bratty attitude, do I read what she wrote on the back of her test.

My favorite home remedy for a cough and sore throat is a cup of chamomile tea with honey and lemon. I suggest Yogi Organic brand tea for best results. I hope you feel better soon.

I snap my jaw shut, hardly aware that it was hanging open. She wrote a note telling me about tea. For my cough that wasn't a cough. Why the hell would she do that? And why am I getting my phone out to order five boxes of Yogi Organic chamomile tea to be delivered to my home tomorrow?

The rest of class drags on, but eventually, everyone finishes their test. I was planning to get a few things done after class, but I can't stand to be in this building for one more fucking minute. Miss Robbins is wearing the threads of my sanity thin. It's only a matter of time before I break.

Three hours later I'm in my car calling my best friend to complain about the fundraiser I'm going to.

"Hello? Reed? Are you there?"

"Dylan? Is that you? Sorry Kayla's being a little fussy right now."

"It's okay man, is this a bad time?"

"Every time is a bad time," he says exasperatedly.

"How is Kayla doing?"

"Other than screaming, crying, throwing temper tantrums, and drawing all over everything, she's great." Reed sighs, the sound low and defeated. "I'm sorry, I'm just tired."

"I can imagine. I would have no idea what to do with a kid."

"Yeah, well, clearly I'm not doing so great either. I don't know how my sister did it."

"Have you thought of hiring a nanny?"

"No." His voice is harsh, but I'm not sure why. "My sister wanted me to take care of her daughter, and that's exactly what I'm going to do."

"You'd still be raising her, you would just have some extra help." Reed grunts on the other end of the line, and I know I've overstepped. "I'm not telling you what to do, just worried about you."

Reed sighs again, and it sounds like he's deflating. "I know, I'm sorry I snapped. I'm just so stressed, and I'm drowning. But that's not why you called. What's up?"

"I'm on my way to the fundraiser," I say with as much enthusiasm as I can muster up, which is to say, not much. "I wanted to check in and see if there was anything you needed me to do specifically."

"Just the usual, schmooze, make jokes, try not to piss anyone off." He laughs at his own joke, and I roll my eyes. "Oh yeah, Senator Robbins is going to be there, too. It would be good for our prized professor to brush shoulders with him, you know, leave a good impression."

I groan and roll my shoulders, already feeling the tension creep up. "I hate leaving good impressions," I grumble. "Wait, did you say Senator Robbins?" Dammit was that too obvious? I shouldn't care. It shouldn't matter. Still, I'd be lying if I said I wasn't excited about the chance to see

Sarah so soon. Today is Thursday, which means the next chance I get to see her is in five days. Apparently, that's too long.

A loud pterodactyl screech sounds from the other side of the line, and I pull my phone away from my ear to save my eardrums.

"Yes, Senator Robbins. I'm sorry Dylan, I have to go. I think Kayla is about to burn down the house."

"Good luck, Reed." The phone disconnects before I even finish my sentence. Poor guy.

I pull into the winery where the fundraiser is being held, already wishing I could be home. My stomach swirls with dread and disappointment as I trudge up the fancy steps into the main hall. Try as I might to ignore it, a thread of excitement weaves its way into my thoughts. I tell myself it's not because I'm going to see Sarah, but I know it's a lie. It's not like anything is going to happen. I'm just going to look. Look and not touch.

Yeah fucking right.

I'm greeted at the door by an underpaid waiter who offers me alcohol and finger foods. I brushed past him in search of one person only. Sarah Robbins. I barely notice the multiple chandeliers, diamond crusted serving dishes, and mood lighting. Everything is over-the-top, as per usual at these events. It doesn't matter, though. I need my Sarah fix.

Reed's words come flooding back into my mind that I need to "schmooze" and seek out the senator, *not his daughter*, to impress.

I slow down, not realizing I was practically running, and grab a glass of champagne from the next waiter I see standing in the corner. I take two measured breaths and count my steps, trying to appear professional, like the lauded Professor I am.

After ten minutes of mingling, I am bored out of my fucking mind. I sip my champagne, wanting to make it last as long as possible. I'm not one to drink heavily, since I've seen enough of how alcohol can destroy a man and his family. Plus, if I get enough alcohol in my system, who knows if I would be able to hold back my feelings for Miss Robbins.

I've nearly convinced myself that Sarah isn't here, and I have nothing to worry about, but then I get a glimpse of her heart-stopping figure. God, I thought she was beautiful in her everyday leggings and loose fitting tops. But now? In a tight black cocktail dress?

My insatiable appetite for her somehow grows more desperate, as jealous rage bubbles up from my core. Did her father see her in that dress? Did he really let her go out looking like this?

I want to peel the damn thing off of her and admire her curves. At the same time, I want to throw a blanket around her, toss her over my shoulder, and take her home so no one can see her. She's *mine*, dammit.

I'm frozen in place, but my eyes wander up and down her hills and valleys, taking in every inch of her decadent body. Her black hair is twisted up in an elegant updo, with perfectly curled wisps softly framing her face. Sarah doesn't normally wear makeup to class, but today she has gray and blue eyeshadow that make her eyes pop. And her lips. Jesus, they're lined with dark red lipstick, and all I can think about is how sexy she would look with them wrapped around my cock.

The silky black material hugs her hips before flaring out into several layers of sparkling black tulle. The sweetheart top dives in between her breasts, showcasing what's mine and mine alone. I stand here practically gaping at the voluptuous woman across the room.

She looks a little lost, and it's the first time I've seen her vulnerable. Sarah tugs the bottom of her dress down, but it only serves to show more of her tempting chest. She notices this too, and attempts to fix the situation by pulling up on her top as well. The end result is that the dress is just too damn small for her. She looks incredible, but also uncomfortable, and I wonder why she chose this outfit.

My eyes wander down her long legs, stopping at the stilettos she's wearing, which make her ass look great but have to be killing her feet. The poor girl shuffles her weight from side to side and I can tell she's already in pain. A surge of protectiveness that I hardly recognize sweeps through my body, jarring me out of my paralysis. I need to get to her. I need to take her shoes off and rub her feet and make sure she never hurts again.

What is wrong with me? How can I want to fuck her in every dirty way imaginable, and also wrap her up in a fuzzy blanket and cradle her until she falls asleep?

My feet start moving before my brain can catch up, and I'm carried toward her, drawn like a magnet. My girl hasn't noticed me yet, but right before I reach her, a hand wraps around her bicep and tugs her off to the side. I swallow back and growl, not wanting to cause a scene, but needing to get this fucker's hands off of my property.

I don't have time to wrestle with that thought, as I follow the older man and Sarah down to the wine cellar.

The two of them go behind a shelf of French wines from the 1970s, and I sneak in as well, sticking to the side of the room in the shadows. I'm not sure what's happening, all I know is I need to be here for Sarah. My gut is never wrong, and I can tell something isn't right.

"Dad, let go." Sarah shakes off her father's grip on her bicep, and rubs her arm. My fists tighten at the thought of her father causing her harm. I'm still not sure what's going on, so I swallow down my anger and stay quiet.

"Where is your new necklace? I bought it specifically for tonight. I wanted you to show it off."

"I thought the necklace was for last week's dinner. What does it matter anyway?"

Her father, Senator Robbins, is every bit the asshole the media portrays him to be. I don't like the way he's talking to his daughter. I don't like the way he's treating her, and I sure as hell don't like the way he's touching her.

"I don't ask much from you, Sarah. I pay for your education, your housing, and your wardrobe. So when I ask you to show up in the fifteen hundred dollar necklace I got for you, and play nice with the Erickson twins, I expect you to do just that. And I expect you to do it without complaining."

"I didn't ask for the necklace," Sarah counters. She crosses her arms over her chest in a protective stance. "I didn't ask for the penthouse, either. I definitely didn't ask for dresses two sizes too small, or heels six inches too tall. I've told you that the clothes the stylist picked out make me feel uncomfortable.

What? Her father dressed her? I'm liking this man less and less.

"Stop it," her father hisses. "You ungrateful little..."

I'm half a second away from lunging at the sorry motherfucker, but he wisely stops himself from completing that sentence.

"Look," he says with a sigh. "I don't have time for your attitude right now. This is our deal. You still want to graduate with your nursing degree? Then get out there and make the Erikson twins feel good."

Sarah gapes at her father, as do I. Is he suggesting...?

"Oh my God, dad. What are you saying?" She looks horrified, and I take a step out from behind the shadows, ready to snatch my little princess away and then punch her father in the fucking balls.

"I'm not a monster, Jesus," he growls. "You don't have to fuck them, just flirt with them."

"But—"

"It's not like you could attract that kind of attention anyway," he mutters. "Lose a few pounds, then maybe..." he trails off and shakes his head. What the actual fuck is wrong with this man?

I've seen Sarah's anger and heard her snappy comebacks several times this semester, so I'm waiting for her response. Surely, she'll tear him apart limb from limb for treating her like this. I'll finish whatever she starts, but she deserves this moment to take the Senator down a peg.

Instead, to my horror, Sarah hangs her head. Her shoulders drop and her stance changes from defensive to defeated. I barely hear her soft sniffling, but it rips my heart in two.

"Go to the restroom and get yourself together," Senator Robbins scolds. "The Erikson's are all lined up to give my campaign a big donation, so I need you to play your part and keep the twins entertained while their father and I talk business."

That's it. I've had enough of this shit. Moving from my hiding spot, I eat up the distance between me and my woman in a matter of three strides. I get there just in time to see her turning her back and scurrying away, leaving me face to face with the infamous Senator Robbins.

"Professor Cole, right?" the Senator asks, holding out his hand. His face immediately twists into a slimy smile, all traces of cruelty toward his daughter long gone.

"Yes," I confirm, gripping his hand a little too tightly and shaking it a little too roughly. I look over his shoulder, hoping for another glance of Sarah. I only see the back door closing, meaning she got away. I'll find her soon. At least she's safe from this asshole.

"Kids," he says, shrugging his shoulders and looking toward the exit his daughter just fled through.

I grunt, dropping his hand before folding my arms over my chest. I half listen to what he's blabbering on about, but mostly, I'm fantasizing about all the ways I can make this man suffer for what he put Sarah through.

Not here, though. I don't need to give Reed another thing to worry about.

When I've spent a respectable amount of time humoring the idiot as he talks about the campaign trail, I excuse myself and head straight for the restrooms. I need to see my little girl and make sure she's okay.

Chapter Four

Sarah

I keep my head down as I push the restroom door open, thankful when I see it's empty. Bracing myself with both palms on the sink, I take a deep breath, trying to hold back the tears.

"Just make it through tonight," I whisper to myself. "Two more hours. I can make it two more hours."

Lifting my head, I stare at my reflection in the mirror. I don't recognize the woman I see. Deep red lipstick, dark eyeshadow, and enough bobby pins in my hair to sink a ship. And this dress... God, it's awful. The stylist dropped it off this morning, insisting it would be perfect for this fundraising event. Perfect for who, I'm not sure. Definitely not me.

Honestly, I don't know if I have the strength to do what my father wants. Flirt? I wouldn't know how to do that even if I wanted to. I've never thought much about boys, and up until my father started dressing me up and parading me around a few years ago, boys never thought about me, either.

It hasn't mattered until tonight. Yes, my dad has set up several "networking dinners" with friends who have sons my age, but it was always so awkward. He didn't outright say he was setting me up, but it doesn't take a genius to figure that out. Up until now, though, my father hasn't pressured me to flirt and play nice, whatever that means.

A sob catches in my throat, and I try to swallow it down. Tears threaten to pour down my cheeks, but I push them back. If I start now, I won't be able to stop, and that would truly be a disaster.

I close my eyes and inhale deeply, gathering all of my stress and tension, then releasing it in one long exhale. Two more slow breaths, and I finally open my eyes, feeling a little more at ease. I run cold water over the insides of my wrists, a trick I learned a few years ago for centering yourself.

"Two more months," I tell myself on repeat. Once I have my nursing degree, I can apply for jobs, get my own apartment, and live life without all the strings attached to my family's money.

Somewhere in the back of my mind and the pit of my stomach, I know my father's control won't just go away once I graduate, but I can't think about that right now. All I can do is focus on getting through college. The rest is a battle for another day.

I open up my small, sequined purse and pull out a tissue. Dabbing it under my eyes, I clean up any hint of tears before blowing my nose in a very unladylike manner. I smirk to myself, even though it's dumb. A tiny act of rebellion that no one will know about. Still, it makes me feel more in control of my situation. I can't change the rules, but I don't have to follow them all the time either.

Squaring my shoulders, I take a final cleansing breath and open the door, bracing myself for the next few hours of torture.

I'm stopped by a wall that was somehow constructed in the few minutes I was in the restroom. Looking up, I inhale sharply as I peer into the golden brown eyes that have haunted my every thought since the semester began.

"Miss Robbins," Professor Cole says, his hands coming down to rest on my shoulders, steadying me.

I shiver at his touch, the way his large, warm hands feel against the soft skin of my exposed shoulders. My spine tingles and I can't seem to breathe as he tears me apart with a single look.

"Professor C-Cole," I stutter out like an idiot. Good lord, I've never been this close to him. He smells like spicy aftershave and mint, and I want to soak it up so I can remember it when I inevitably dream about him tonight.

We stand there, staring at each other for long moments. Slowly, Professor Cole's hands slide up my shoulders, his fingers brushing against the sides of my neck, making my pulse jump and my breath catch. He cradles my face, holding me so gently I think I might cry.

I have to be imagining this, right? Maybe I had a full-blown meltdown in the bathroom and passed out, and this is just some fantasy. That makes more sense than Professor McHottie-slash-rude-asshole looking at me like I'm his salvation.

What could I possibly offer someone in his position anyway? Plus, he's made it clear what he thinks of me. Spoiled, entitled, and mooching off of my parents. Never mind the fact that I'm a good student, I've shown up *early* to every class since that first one, and even gave him my favorite home remedy for a cold!

I try glaring at him. Really, I do. But I'm just so damn tired of having my defenses up all the time. Professor Cole's face softens, his golden eyes prying me wide open until it feels like he's staring at my bruised heart.

His thumbs brush my cheeks, back and forth, back and forth, so tenderly. "Are you okay?" Why does he care? And why do I want to tell him the truth? I squash that thought, nodding my head instead. "Sarah," he warns, that firm tone igniting a flame deep in my core. Oh God, a tingling heat crawls down my spine, landing right between my legs. I press my thighs together, trying to relieve the pressure there.

"Fine," I squeak out. I wince at the weakness in my voice, then clear my throat and try again. "I'm fine. I didn't know you were going to be here." As difficult as it is, I take a step back from the Professor.

His hands drop to his sides, and he clenches his fists before shoving them into his pockets. His eyes never leave mine, however. I know he doesn't believe me, but he has the decency not to call me out on it.

Without thinking, I rest my palms over my cheeks where Professor Cole was holding me. It's like I want to keep that feeling there, sealing his touch into my skin so I can remember it when I'm lonely. Realizing how dumb I must look, I drop my hands and hold them behind my back.

He doesn't say anything, his strong jaw and stoic expression giving nothing away. "I, um… I'm here to support my father," I say, stumbling over the last word.

It might just be my imagination again, but I swear Professor Cole's eyes harden and shoulders tense at the mention of my dad. Still, he says nothing. I feel vulnerable under his gaze, not to mention exposed in my too-short, too-tight dress.

I excuse myself and push past the Professor, hoping some space will clear my head and help me focus on surviving the evening. I wasn't expecting him to be here, and now I feel even more awkward about the task my father set out for me. I don't know why, but it feels like I'm being unfaithful to Professor Cole. Crazy, I know. That's why I need to get lost in the crowd and find the Erikson twins.

Not looking back, I weave my way through the growing number of people mulling about the expansive room. I grab a glass of champagne, though I have no intention of drinking it. I just need to look the part.

Leaning against a side table, I scan the room for the Eriksons, spotting their spiky, bleach-blond hair right away. These two take the whole twin thing to the next level. Rumor has it, they like to play tricks on their conquests, switching places on dates and even in the bedroom. Or so I'm told. I've never been in their sights, and I'm thankful for that. Except now, I'm walking straight into the lion's den.

Brandon and Bryce Erikson are up at the bar, loading up on mixed drinks. Great. So they'll be tipsy, tricky, and handsy, no doubt. Will my father really notice if I just slip out without talking to them?

Of course, he will. He always knows. And I'm so close to finishing my education and starting my own life, I can't afford to screw up now. It's just flirting, like my dad said. At the very least, I can go stand by them so my father can look over and see me doing his bidding.

One of the twins, Bryce, I think, turns his head, looking at me over his shoulder. His eyes slide up my body, pausing on my chest before a wicked grin takes over his pinched face. He nudges his brother and whispers something in his ear.

My gut reaction is to flee, wanting to avoid this kind of attention. It takes everything in me to stay rooted in place while the Erikson twins order a third drink and then head my way.

I'm so anxious about what I'm going to say when they get here, I don't notice someone has stepped up next to me, leaning against the same table.

"Don't do this."

Professor Cole's deep, smooth voice rolls over me, blanketing me in warmth and safety. Why I feel invincible when he's next to me is a mystery, but I'll take strength anywhere I can get it at this point.

"Do what?" I ask, trying to keep my voice light. He can't possibly know what I'm up to. I dart my eyes in his direction, startled by how close he is. His normally amber eyes turn deep brown as he narrows them at me.

Before he gets a chance to answer, Bryce and Brandon come to a stumbling stop in front of me.

"Hey there," Bryce slurs. This soiree has only been going on for an hour and he's already drunk. Wonderful.

"Haven't seen you before," Brandon adds, leaning into my personal space.

Professor Cole wraps his hand around Brandon's shoulder and pushes him backward. "Step back," he growls. I look up at him, furrowing my brows. Why does he care? Why is he still here?

"Whoa, dude," Brandon whines.

"Yeah, chill out," Bryce chimes in. "We were just checking this pretty little thing out. She was giving us the eyes. You know, the *eyes.*" Bryce wiggles his eyebrows, and I curl in on myself.

"I think you misunderstood," I start, hoping to somehow get this situation under control.

"Come on, give us a chance. You're... bigger than the women we normally go for, but it might be fun. What do you think? Two guys who can–"

"Enough!" Professor Cole snarls.

"It's okay," I say in my calmest voice. I put my hands up, palms out, trying to placate everyone. How did I end up in this mess? Why is my professor acting this way? Almost as if he's... jealous. Is that it? No way. But what if...

"Yeah, you heard the lady," Bryce spits out. "Everything is okay. Let's just dance and see where things go.

I look up at Professor Cole, his golden eyes latching on to mine. With a subtle shake of his head, I know he's not pleased with me considering Bryce's offer. For some reason, that makes me want to test this new boundary. I want to see how far he'll go to keep me all to himself. If that's even what's happening, which it probably isn't.

"Well, maybe just one–"

"Fetch me a drink," Professor Cole grunts, shoving several hundred dollar bills into Bryce's hands. The idiot looks at the money, then back at the professor. "You too," he growls, looking at Brandon.

"Uh..."

"Now," he says, his voice low and deadly. I nearly melt into a puddle at the dark tone he's aiming at the Erikson twins. No one has ever defended me or chased away threats. I can't quite say how it makes me feel, or what I'm supposed to do now that I know what it's like to be protected.

The two boys take the hint and scramble off, getting lost in the sea of wealthy socialites.

"You're never going to see that money again, Professor," I say, breaking the tense silence.

Professor Cole places his hand on the small of my back, slowly inching up my spine. My knees wobble and I sway closer to the tall, enigmatic man next to me. His fingers tangle in my hair, sending a few bobby pins falling to the ground as he gathers my tresses in his fist.

I gasp softly when he tugs, pulling my head back in a firm but gentle grip. I stare up at him, his intense amber eyes glowing as they bore into mine. I can feel his labored breaths tickle my lips and across my cheeks, making me swallow hard.

"I don't give a fuck about the money," he grits out.

I chew on my bottom lip, not sure what's happening between us, just that I never want it to end. The roar of the party is muted as I sink into this moment with the Professor. My sex is pulsing, my clit throbbing in time with my frantic heartbeat. He's so in control, so in charge of my every move. I'm aware of every nerve in my body, each one lighting up and sizzling at his touch.

"Then why...?"

My words are caught in my throat as Professor Cole dips his head, his lips brushing against my cheek. I inhale sharply, holding my breath. Is this happening? Anyone could see us. My *father* could see us. What is he doing? And why is that so hot?

"Call me Dylan," he murmurs into the shell of my ear.

"Dylan," I whisper. He groans, the sound causing me to drench my panties. Is he really that affected by me? Impossible. "Why–"

"They weren't worthy of you."

I'm shocked and confused by his words. Maybe that's why I blurt out, "And you are?"

Dylan tightens his hold on my hair, the slight sting only heightening my arousal. He's so damn big, so all-consuming, so masculine and sure of himself. I want him to be sure of me, too. I want him to tell me he'll always have my back, he'll always come to my rescue. He might have me trapped right now, but there's no place I'd rather be.

"No," he says with a scowl. I raise my eyebrows in surprise. I wasn't expecting that answer. Dylan tilts my head to the side, exposing my neck. A breathy moan leaves my lips as his teeth scrape against my tender flesh, stopping to nip at my pulse point. "Be a good girl and don't talk to those fuckers ever again."

I ignore the lightning flashing through my body, and the dull ache it leaves behind when he calls me a good girl. Holy crap. I want to be his good girl. I want his praise. God, I'm messed up.

"But my dad..."

"Is an asshole," he grunts into the side of my neck. "Maybe you need a new one."

All the air leaves my lungs, and my legs turn to jelly. I somehow know he doesn't want to be my father figure. He wants to be my... Daddy?

As soon as the thought crosses my mind, my face heats up and I need to lean against Dylan to keep my balance.

"Would you like that, little girl?"

His voice is rougher now, like he's barely holding on. We're in public, at a freaking fundraiser for the college, and my own father is wandering around, probably looking for me. And yet... all I can think about is getting down on my knees and pleasing this man in every possible way.

"I..."

"I'm sure Professor Cole is around here somewhere," a voice bellows from somewhere off to the side. "I was just talking to him in the wine cellar."

I recognize my father's tone, and then the pieces fall into place. Did Dylan hear what my dad said in the cellar? Oh my God, does Dylan feel sorry for me? Does he think I'm some pathetic damsel who needs saving? Maybe he does want to be my father figure and nothing more.

"Professor Cole," I whisper.

He looks across the room, then back at me, frustration etched in his features. Dylan presses a kiss to my temple, the sweet, confusing gesture almost more than I can handle. I have a hundred questions, a thousand thoughts, and a million desires I never even knew existed.

Dylan releases my hair, which is surely a mess by now, letting his fingers trail down my side until they dive into my purse. It all happens so quickly, I don't have time to react. Professor Cole grabs my phone, then loops his fingers around my right wrist, bringing my thumb up to the screen to unlock it.

I watch silently as he types his number into my contacts, then calls himself. A second later, he tucks my phone back into my purse, gives me a final look, then walks away.

What the hell was that?

Chapter Five

Dylan

I don't know what the fuck I was thinking at the fundraiser. I shouldn't have given her my number. Maybe then, I wouldn't have spent the last two days staring at my damn phone, waiting for it to light up with a text from Sarah.

I fill my mug with hot water, then add a bag of chamomile tea, bobbing it up and down to distribute the flavor. My throat doesn't hurt, but every part of me *aches* for another glimpse of my princess. I watch the water turn from clear to a cloudy yellow, then take a sip, savoring every second.

Closing my eyes, I picture starting every Sunday morning like this, with one major change. My little girl would be right here next to me, curled up on my lap while we sip tea together on the couch. Relaxing into the fantasy, I lean my head back and let the feeling of contentment wash over me.

I have no doubt a life with Sarah would never be boring. The witty woman full of sass would keep me on my toes, day and night. And I would sweep my princess off of her feet every damn time, coaxing her lips to part for me as I give us what we both need.

My obsession is more than just physical. More than her sweet blush and quick comebacks. It's more than anything I've ever experienced, more than I ever thought possible. I want to wrap my arms around Sarah and protect her from the whole damn world. I want her to know she's safe with me and that I'll do whatever it takes to help her reach her dreams. Her father's generosity comes with a million strings attached, but I want to show my little girl I'll give her everything just for being her. It would be my joy and honor to support her, cherish her, and watch her reach every one of her goals.

"Fuck," I mutter to myself as I run a hand through my messy hair. Sarah's got me all twisted up, inside and out. I can't even think her name without my heart rioting in my chest and my dick pressing uncomfortably against my zipper.

I'm not sure exactly when my carnal thoughts turned so... paternal. Not once in my whole life have I ever thought about being someone's Daddy. I hardly know what that entails, only that what I feel for Sarah is pure, a little messed up, but perfect.

So why the hell hasn't she texted me yet? Can't she feel it, too?

I finish the rest of my tea, setting the mug down on the table a little too forcefully. The ceramic chips, leaving a scratch on the oak side table. "Great," I mumble. I need to chill out. Take a beat. Gather my thoughts before I go completely insane.

It's already too late, though. I'm in too deep. Drowning in the memory of her silky locks tangled in my fingers, her soft skin beneath my lips, and her breathy moan as I held her close. I've replayed every second of our last encounter at least a thousand times in the two days we've been apart.

Jumping up off the couch, I stalk toward the basement, hoping a brutal workout in my home gym will do me some good. I need some way to get this tension out of my body, though I have a feeling there's only one cure for my madness; Sarah Robbins, under me, over me, surrounding me with her sinful body and sweet sighs.

After boxing, sprinting, weight lifting, and soaking my sore muscles in my hot tub, I resigned to my home office to grade papers. The way things have been going with my concentration lately, it'll take me the rest of the evening to get through even one class.

Shuffling through yet another mess of tests, I see Sarah's name scribbled on one of the papers. I pull it from the stack, holding it in front of me like it's a rare, precious document. Jesus Christ, in my mind, it is. I flip it over, rereading her note about the tea, then glance over her answers.

Of course, she nailed the technical questions about names and dates. I've learned that my princess is very practical, which makes sense considering her chosen field of study. I didn't expect her to be interested in nursing, but I can see it now. She has a big heart, and despite her outward sass, I know it's tender. The way her father took advantage of her at the fundraiser made that crystal clear. I hate thinking about what other shit he's put her through.

I skim over the more abstract questions, the ones asking about the application of certain philosophical concepts. It's one thing to know Descartes made the famous statement, "I think, therefore, I am," but something else entirely to realize the implications of mind-body dualism in everyday life.

Sarah is a good student, of that, there's no doubt. I can tell she's trying to explore these ideas in the essay portion of the test, but she's not digging deep enough. Even so, I get caught up in her words, her struggle, her mindset as she wrote out this test.

It's fascinating, following her train of thought, and seeing where she can't quite make the existential leap into the unknown. Sarah is comfortable with numbers, dates, and facts, but wading into murky waters isn't her style. She wants control, but that's just because she doesn't know how freeing it can be to surrender.

I mark her paper with an 87%, a solid B. I'm still an asshole for wanting to bend my student over my lap and spank her before sinking inside her over and over, but at least I've given her an honest grade. It might not mean much in the long run, but it will help me sleep a little easier at night. I've crossed a lot of boundaries, and I plan on crossing a lot more, but I'd never disrespect my woman by making her feel cheap or treating her like she's sleeping her way through her education. Sarah is nothing like that.

Staring at the damn test, my fingers twitch, then my hand moves on its own, grabbing my phone off the desk. I scroll through my contacts, hoving over Sarah's number. I put her in as Princess, which satisfies some dark part of me I didn't know existed until now.

I shouldn't text her. I know this. I should set my phone down, or hell, lock it in a drawer and leave for the evening.

Instead, agonize over which words to use, forgetting how to put them together in a coherent sentence. In the end, I go with, **I trust that you're having a good evening.**

As soon as I hit send, I want to pluck the words out of the screen and flush them down the toilet. I stand up, pacing back and forth as Istare at my phone. What is she supposed to say to that? It wasn't even a question. Why didn't I...

My thoughts cease as three little bubbles pop up on screen. I hold my breath, waiting for her to put me out of my misery.

Princess: I trust that you're bored if you're texting me.

I cough out a laugh, all the nerves leaving my body at once as I collapse back into my chair.

Me: That's not an answer.

Princess: You didn't ask me a question.

Princess: ...Daddy.

I groan, biting my lip to stave off the flood of arousal washing over me. I set my contact name to Daddy, for some goddamn reason. It was spur of the moment. I was rattled after touching her, teasing her, and then being ripped away from her.

Me: Tell me what you're doing, Princess.

Princess: That's not a question either.

Me: Do you like tormenting me, little girl?

Princess: Only as much as you like tormenting me.

Me: Are you always this difficult?

I grin at our back and forth, but then frown when she doesn't respond. Shit. Did I offend her? I thought we were flirting. Kind of. I don't know. Jesus, it's been years since I've done anything remotely resembling flirting, and never with anyone I want so desperately.

Five minutes go by, then ten. After twenty minutes, I'm about ready to throw my phone into the washing machine and go another round with the punching bag. But then my phone dings with an incoming text.

Princess: Sorry, I didn't mean to ghost you. I'm at a stupid dinner with my family.

A vision of her father's ugly, bloated mug fills my head, and I growl at the memory of how he treated her.

Me: Are you okay? Where are you at?

Princess: Are you going to be my knight in shining armor?

Me: Yes.

Princess: OMG, I was kidding! Lighten up, Professor.

Me: What's my name?

Princess: Awfully demanding today, aren't we?

Me: You don't know the half of it.

Me: Tell me you're okay. I'm losing my shit, Princess.

Was that too much? Probably. All of this is too much. I shouldn't be texting her. I shouldn't be thinking about her every second of every day. I most definitely shouldn't be planning to do so much more.

Princess: I'm okay.

Me: Where are you?

Princess: Like I said, just a stuffy dinner with my mom, dad, and their friends who just so happen to have a son my age.

I grip my phone so hard, the plastic cracks under the pressure. Easing up a bit, I take a deep breath and try to remain level headed. No easy task, considering some sleazy, punk ass kid is sitting across from *my* little girl, probably eyeing her up in whatever horrible dress her family made her wear. No, I'm not liking this one bit. Still, I have to play it cool, or else risk looking even crazier than I am.

Me: Give me the address right the fuck now.

Well, so much for playing it cool.

Princess: And you'll do what? Storm in here and whisk me away?

Me: Something like that.

Princess: Life doesn't work that way.

Me: It could. Let me prove it to you.

Bubbles appear, disappear, then appear again, only to cease after a few seconds.

Several minutes go by, followed by several more. I resume my pacing, trying to figure out what I'm going to do if she doesn't respond. There are a few upscale restaurants near campus, so I could start looking there. I have the personal number of several Michelin star chefs in the area, which should help me in my search. Once I find her, and I *will* find my little girl, I'm going to teach her a lesson about ignoring me, especially when it comes to her safety.

I throw on my jacket, grab my keys, and pull up the number for Chef Gonzolaz, deciding to start there first. Right before I connect the call, a text from Sarah pops up.

Princess: We're at Les Amis.

Another text comes in immediately, followed by another.

Princess: I don't know why I told you that.

Princess: What are we doing?

Me: Wait ten minutes, then head to the ladies room.

Me: We're doing what we've both wanted since you first walked into class late.

Princess: Oh my god, it was two minutes!

I smirk as I float out to my car.

Me: Your punishment will last at least five times as long.

With that, I rev the engine and tear off down the road, toward Les Amis.

I get there in under eight minutes, parking my car in the back and sprinting toward the door. I manage to get my breathing under control by the time I step up to the maître d', letting her know I'm meeting someone who has already been seated. She doesn't question my authoritative tone, letting me slip past her into the seating area.

I make a beeline to the back, straight for the dimly-lit hallway leading to the restrooms.

There, leaning against the wall in a green silk wrap dress, is my princess. She's twisting her hands nervously, anxiety rolling off of her as she fidgets from side to side. God, it's only been a few days since I've seen her, but my little girl is absolutely gorgeous.

Her head tips up, and those brilliant teal eyes find mine, equal parts excited and apprehensive. She nibbles her bottom lip before licking away the sting.

The sight of her little pink tongue is my breaking point.

I close the distance between us, grabbing Sarah's hand and pulling her into the ladies room. It's empty, though I don't think anything would stop me from claiming her lips for the first time.

"What are—"

I cut her off by leaning her against the closed door and devouring her mouth. She opens for me and sucks on my tongue, making me growl. My hands grasp the sides of her neck, my thumbs caressing her jawline as I tilt her head to the side to deepen our kiss.

It's a frantic, desperate kiss, the kind that pulls you under and threatens the very limits of your sanity. I've never felt this much need, this much desire for anyone in my goddamn life, and I'm not sure what to do about it. The fact that she wants this as much as I do is a major fucking turn on.

When we finally break for air, I rest my forehead on hers. "Sarah," I pant, running my eyes up and down her body.

"Daddy..." she manages to say in between breaths.

Jesus, I shouldn't love it when she calls me that, but I do.

I want to rip her clothes off and ram my ten inches into her tight, silky heat, but this isn't the time nor the place. I'll just have to give her a few orgasms with my mouth.

I take her lips one more time, sweeping my tongue inside and gliding it along the roof of her mouth. My Sarah moans so sweetly, so softly for me. When I pull back, her eyes are clouded over with lust. Goddamn, my baby girl looks good like this.

Leaning forward, I ghost my lips up and down her neck, breathing in her sweet scent and tickling her sensitive flesh. When she's trembling at my touch, I whisper into the shell of her ear, "Are you ready for your punishment, naughty little girl?"

"Wh-what?" she gasps. "I thought y-you were k-kidding."

"I never joke about discipline, princess," I murmur, kissing down the side of her neck. "I have a feeling you'll like your punishment. I know I will."

Sarah's breath catches as she shivers in my arms. I spin her around so she's bracing herself against the wall of the bathroom. I place one hand on her hip, while the other slides up her back, pushing her forward so she's presenting her ass so beautifully to me.

I've never had this urge, this desire, this fucking insane, insatiable need to spank someone. Never thought about it until Sarah, but she needs it. I need it. We need this moment, and every moment after. This is just the beginning.

Sarah looks at me over her shoulder, her pouty lips opening to give me some sass, I just know it. Before she can get a single word out, I flip the hem of her dress over her hips, exposing her creamy cheeks, barely covered by a tiny pair of black lace panties.

"Who are these for?" I growl, slipping my hand into the waistband and tugging them down.

"N-No one," Sarah pants, her legs spreading as I kick her feet apart, stretching her lace panties until they are tight around her upper thighs.

"Don't lie to me, princess," I warn, barely grazing the tips of my fingers over her smooth skin.

Sarah shakes her head, then looks back at me. Her clear blue eyes hold agonizing desire, mixed with a raw vulnerability that nearly has me falling to my knees. Whatever she's about to tell me is important, and I need her to know she can trust me.

"I've... I've never, um..."

I quirk an eyebrow up at her, not sure where she's going with this. I trace the lines of her curved cheeks, down the insides of her thighs, barely grazing her soaking wet slit before repeating the path. Sarah lets out a soft whimper, her entire body trembling as I work her up. I'm barely touching her, and she's ready to go off. It's almost too much to take, too perfect to be true. And then she finishes her sentence.

"I've never done this before." Her voice is hardly above a whisper, but I pause, considering her words.

"We'll learn together," I reassure her, resuming my steady strokes all around her thighs, ass, and lower back. "I've never been anyone's Daddy. Never wanted to. Never thought about it. But it feels right, doesn't it?" I hold my breath, waiting for her response.

Sarah nods her head, and I exhale all of my tension in one long sigh.

"But that's not... I mean, I've never done *any* of this." Those blue eyes focus back on mine, and I can hardly believe what my little girl is telling me. I knew she was precious, perfect, and inexperienced. But I had no idea she was a virgin.

I'm not a caveman, but my obsession with this woman has somehow doubled, knowing I'm the only man who will bring her pleasure. I'm the only one who will know what she tastes like, what she feels like, what she sounds like as she's coming around my cock, screaming my name.

"I-I..." Sarah stutters out, slamming her eyes shut. "I don't know why I said that," she mumbles. "Oh my god, I'm such a freak."

That snaps me out of my lustful daze.

I smack her left cheek lightly, my cock twitching when she jumps in surprise. "First rule. No talking bad about yourself, princess." I spank her again, a little bit harder this time. "You're not a freak. You're my little girl. You saved yourself for Daddy, isn't that right?"

I have no idea where these words are coming from, but I can't stop. It's this connection between us, this unnamable force that has drawn out my dark and twisted desires.

"Yes," she whispers.

"Yes, who?" I demand, gripping her cheek and kneading the soft flesh.

"Yes, Daddy. I was waiting for you."

"Good girl," I groan, dipping my fingers into her juicy little slit. Sarah clenches around me, her arousal drenching my hand as I work her clit in relentless circles. My princess sags against the wall as I rub her pussy over and over, spasming each time I play with her bundle of nerves.

She inhales sharply, her muscles drawing up tight while her cunt pulses and her cream pools in my hand. Right before she's thrown over the edge into complete bliss, I withdraw my hand and land three blows to her ass, growling as it turns pink and then red.

"Professor!" she exclaims, her entire body like a livewire, sparking to life with every single touch.

"Ah, that's not my name, is it, princess? Not when we're like this."

Sarah whimpers and shakes her head, rocking her hips against me, silently begging me to continue.

"Please, Daddy. I need... I think I need more."

I don't waste any time giving my little girl what she asked for.

Withdrawing my hand from her center, I wipe her cum all over her rounded cheeks, watching her skin glisten so beautifully for me. My little girl is surrendering herself to me, and I'll make sure she never regrets it.

"Count," I growl before lifting my hand and spanking her slick ass once.

"One," Sarah squeaks out, having trouble catching her breath. I reel back and give her more, alternating cheeks, until she reaches ten.

I bury my face into the back of her neck, inhaling her sugary scent mixed with sweat, the smell in of itself enough to make me addicted. I smooth one hand over her sore bottom while the other slides up her front, cupping her generous breast.

"That what you needed, princess? Needed Daddy to remind you who you belong to? Who is in control?"

Sarah nods, but won't look at me. I take a step back and then spin her around, gathering up my precious girl into my arms. She tucks herself into my embrace, clinging to me as her curvy body shivers.

"Yes," she murmurs, the sound muffled from where her face is buried in my shirt.

"Are you okay, Sarah? God, I... I've never done that either, and if I hurt you..."

"I'm good," she insists, popping her head up to look at me. Her cheeks are pink, her eyes are bright, and she's nibbling her bottom lip again, barely suppressing a smile.

"Good," I say with a nod. "You were such a good girl for your punishment," I praise her. "Now it's time for your reward."

"What...?"

I answer her question by pulling her panties all the way off. In one swift move, she's naked from the waist down, and I'm kneeling before her. I don't give her time to protest or question my actions as I throw one of her legs over my shoulder and lick her slit from bottom to top, making her tremble in my hands.

I suck on every part of her perfect pussy, letting her juices drip down my chin. She's marking me with her flavor. Nothing and no one will ever give me this. She's the one, I know it now more than ever. She's worth the risk, worth my career, worth every single penny in my bloated bank account. I'd give it all up for one more taste.

I lift Sarah's other leg to rest on my shoulder, opening her up even more for me. I pin her to the wall using my body, my hands on her hips.

She grips my hair and pulls as I eat her to a drenching orgasm. Sarah bucks against my mouth, coming hard and fast.

I lick her through it, adding my finger into her dripping entrance.

"Please, please, that's...I can't come again..."

Her pained pleas only spur me on. I drop my finger from her tight hole and trade it for my tongue, fucking her this way until she comes again. I let go of her hip and bring one hand down on her ass, smacking her once, twice, three times, until she's squirting into my mouth with another release, giving me what I need.

I growl into her soaking cunt, her juices driving me to the point of madness. I want more, but I know our time is up. This is far from over, though. We've only just begun.

"Fuck, Dylan, ohmygod...Daddy," she breathes out as she comes down from her high.

Sarah slumps against me, her body limp, eyes closed. I carefully set her legs back down and lean her against the wall for support while I stand up. I wrap my arms around her and kiss her soft, welcoming lips, letting her taste her own release.

She breaks the kiss and licks me clean. Fucking Christ.

I hold her until she regains her strength, and then I help her get dressed. When she's all put back together, Sarah looks up at me through her long lashes, still flushed from her orgasms.

"Beautiful," I whisper, kissing her temple and the top of her head. "Thank you for trusting me, princess. That was everything."

Sarah nods, but her eyes fall, breaking contact with me. "I should probably get back..."

I snarl, not liking the idea of her leaving my side. Ever.

The softest, sweetest giggle falls from her lips, and I can't help the smile taking over my features at the sound. "I can't just disappear," she says exasperatedly.

"Yes, you can. You're an adult."

She sighs, placing a kiss over my heart before taking a step back. "It's not that simple."

"Nothing about this is simple," I agree. I want to push the matter, tell her she doesn't have to live like that anymore. But, I know it's a lot for her to take in right now. Both of our worlds have permanently changed after what we just shared. I don't want to scare her off. "But we can discuss that later."

My little girl nods, tucking her hair behind her ear. I loop my fingers around her wrist, pulling it to my lips and turning it over so I can kiss her there. Leaning down, I brush my lips against her forehead and nose, then give her the tiniest peck on the lips.

"Be at my place in twenty minutes, princess. Will that be enough time to get out of this miserable restaurant?"

"I don't even know where you live!"

"That's not a no," I tease, lifting an eyebrow. "Besides, I put my address in your phone the night I gave you my number. I wanted you to always be able to find me and to have a safe haven from the world."

"Safe haven," she whispers. "I've never had that."

The honesty and longing dripping from her words have me wrapping her up in my arms once again. "You do now, Sarah. I promise to always take care of you. Do you believe me?"

"Yes," she answers automatically.

"Good girl." I give her one last squeeze, then step away. "Twenty minutes," I tell her before exiting the bathroom. Looking at my sexy little goddess, I fight the urge to throw her over my shoulder and run away with her for good. She needs to come to me. I need her to choose me, choose us.

"Twenty minutes," she confirms, giving me a sly smile.

Twenty goddamn minutes. And then she's mine.

Chapter Six

Sarah

I pull into the driveway of a modern-looking cabin with a wrap around porch, tall bay windows, and a forest green front door. Turning off the car, I rest my head on the steering wheel and take a calming breath.

My heart is pounding and my legs are still shaking from what happened back at the restaurant. I mean, what even *was* that? And what does it say about me that I liked it so much?

If you told me a few months ago I'd be bending over for my professor, begging him to spank me harder, I'd surely have laughed so hard I'd choke. But what we shared was beyond anything I knew existed.

Yes, the act of surrender and show of control was hot as fuck, but there was something else underneath the sexual tension. It wasn't just a fettish or for shock value, I needed his strong hand, his rough voice, and the way he held me so tenderly after. We connected on a level too deep and confusing to name, but I know he felt it too.

I managed to fake a stomach ache when I got back to the dinner table, and my father was more willing to believe me since I was gone for so long. He'd have a stroke if he knew what I was really doing, and who I was doing it with.

The entire drive over to Dylan's house, I've tried coming to terms with what happened, and more importantly, where we go from here. I can't seem to hang on to a single thought, however. My mind has been racing ever since Dylan left me in the restroom. I'll admit, it sucked not to be able to snuggle up in bed with him after the intensity of my orgasms, but maybe that's why he wants me to be at his house. A girl can hope.

Checking the clock on my dashboard, I see it's been almost twenty minutes on the dot from when Dylan told me to show up. Part of me wants to sit out here for a little bit longer and see what he does if I'm late, but mostly, I just want to be in his arms again.

Gathering up the last of my courage, I step out of the car and walk up to the front door. I lift my hand to knock, but before I get the chance, the door swings open, and I'm being pulled inside.

"Missed you," Dylan murmurs before shutting the door and pressing me against it. His mouth is on mine in the next second, our tongues tangling as he grinds himself against me. I moan into the kiss, looping my arms around his neck and clinging to him with everything I have.

This pull we have is inexplicable. I want to surrender to his touch, drown in his kisses, and give into anything and everything my Daddy wants to do to me.

Eventually, Dylan leans back, giving me a chance to catch my breath. "Hello to you, too," I tease, gasping for air. His usually stern, stoic face lights up, his lips spreading into a panty-melting grin. Holy hell, I want him to always look at me like that. I've never seen his smile before, and that's probably a good thing. If I thought the tall, dark, and sexy professor was irresistible before, this is a whole new level of hotness to obsess over.

"How are you feeling?" he asks, tucking me into his side as we step further into the living room. I snuggle up against him, loving that he wants to be as close to me as possible.

Dylan sits down on his huge leather couch, pulling me down to sit on his lap. I shriek in surprise, then giggle when he nuzzles into the side of my neck, nipping me there and making me squirm.

"Love that sound," he whispers, brushing the softest kiss against my forehead. Gah, how is he so sweet? This man is ruining me for all other men.

My stomach drops as I think about being with anyone else, ever. It's crazy, I know. I'm sure Dylan will be done with me soon. Oh, god, am I just a conquest for him? Does he do this with a different student every semester?

"Hey," Dylan murmurs. "Where did you just go?"

"I'm in your lap, mister," I say with a smile, even though I feel like I might be sick.

He pinches my arm, then kisses away the sting. "Don't avoid the subject," he says sternly. "What were you just thinking about? I'll know if you're lying to me, princess, so don't even think about it."

Of course, the first thing I think about is lying. Dylan gently cups my chin, tipping my head up to meet his gaze. Those honey-colored eyes are warm and comforting, letting me know I can trust him.

"I was just wondering..." I blow out a breath, not sure how to even voice my thoughts. "What I am to you. I mean, like, what are we doing? And for how long? Am I just one student in a string of many?" I slap my hand over my mouth, hoping to stop the word vomit.

Squeezing my eyes shut, I silently curse myself for letting my insecurities get the best of me. I'm sure all the other girls Professor Cole has been with were just thankful for any amount of attention he gave them, and here I am, practically asking for a marriage proposal before going any further.

"Look at me, princess," Dylan says softly. I shake my head no, feeling my cheeks heat up in embarrassment. I feel his warm fingers wrap around my wrist, pulling my hand away from my mouth. I peek one eye open, watching as he kisses each finger, then places my palm over his heart. "Feel this?" he whispers, covering my hand with his own. I nod. "Need your words, little girl."

"Yes."

"Good," he praises, making my core throb, despite any embarrassment I'm currently experiencing. "Feel how fast it's beating?" I nod. "Only you, Sarah. Only you can make me feel this... exhilarated. I'm obsessed with you, and only you. Never, not in all my years as an educator, have I had an inappropriate relationship with a student."

His words comfort me as well as put a spotlight on our current situation. "Inappropriate," I echo, dying a little bit inside. Of course, it is. I'm not an idiot. Our relationship is on a limited time table.

"Listen to me," Dylan says more forcefully. "I love what we shared earlier. It felt..." he sighs, looking up to the ceiling as if searching for the right words. "Right," he finally says. "Perfect. I've never expressed myself that way, never thought about it. Sarah, hear me when I say I've never done anything with a student, and I've never spanked anyone, never even thought about being someone's Daddy. Hell, it's been over a decade since I've been with anyone. But one look at you..." He trails off, then tucks some of my hair behind my ear before cupping the side of my face. "I'm going to sound crazy, but the first time I saw you, I wanted to fuck you just as much as I wanted to cuddle you."

I gape at him, but then curl my lips up into the cheesiest smile. "You're kind of a big teddy bear, you know that?"

Those golden eyes darken, and Dylan leans forward, trailing kisses up my neck until he's nibbling on my earlobe. "I think we both know I have another side, don't we, little girl?" His voice is deep and filled with need. I squirm in his lap, gasping when I feel a certain part of him harden beneath me. "Fuck, little girl, I want everything with you. Need it. Can I have another taste?"

"Hmm?" I ask distractedly as Dylan continues teasing me with little bites and kisses all over my neck and shoulders.

"Told you I'm obsessed with you," he grunts, more impatiently this time. "I'm starving, princess. Are you going to let Daddy take what he needs from your delicious little pussy?"

"Again?" The word is barely out of my mouth before a strangled growl erupts from Dylan.

I grip his shoulders as he abruptly stands with me in his arms, then kneels on the plush carpet in front of the fireplace I hadn't noticed earlier. He lays my body down, then leans back on his knees, taking in every inch of me.

The fire casts a flickering orange glow over half of his face, highlighting his strong jaw, angled cheekbones, and full lips. The light catches in his eyes, making them glow brighter than the fire in front of us.

Dylan crawls over me, devouring me with one look. I think he's going to kiss me, but instead, he rubs his nose against mine before trailing his lips and nose down my neck, over my collarbone, between my breasts, and lower, lower, lower...

He bunches my dress up past my hips, then nips at the soft flesh of my belly, sending a jolt of electricity to my throbbing clit, followed by a warm rush of wetness dripping out of my pussy. He never gave me my panties back from our rendezvous in the restroom, so I'm completely bare before this incredible man. Dylan takes a deep breath, sliding the rest of the way down my body so he can focus on my pussy.

"I fucking *smell* how much you want me," he growls, spreading my thighs apart and running his nose up and down my slit. I close my eyes, drowning in need and desire. Some animalistic sound rumbles out of Dylan. I can feel his need as it vibrates through me, making my nipples and clit ache. I feel my channel clench as more of my arousal leaks out.

Dylan growls hungrily as he slides his tongue up and down my pussy, parting my folds. I force my eyes open and look down at his muscular body, rippling and flexing as he devours me. It feels like his tongue is everywhere at once – in my entrance, traveling through my folds, swirling around my clit. It's everywhere, and it's consuming me completely. It's all I can focus on. The intense feeling. The wet, smacking sounds. The pressure and heat.

It makes me even hotter knowing he's loving this. The greedy way he's grabbing my ass, the hungry, desperate moans, the eagerness for more. It's all showing me how much pleasure he gets from this. His rough palms slide to the back of my knees and he shoves my legs open wider, pinning them to the floor so he can sit back and stare at me.

Dylan growls and dives back in, licking me with fury, pushing deeper, harder, faster.

I reach down and tangle my fingers in his hair, pulling and pushing him away in equal measure. I can't decide if it's too much or not enough. Not that Dylan gives me a choice in the matter. I gave up control and now I have to trust him to take care of me.

Dylan lifts his head briefly, locking his gaze on mine. God, he looks possessed. Feral, even. Did I really do that to him?

"Yeah, princess," he grunts. "You did this to me. This pussy is unreal."

My cheeks heat up with embarrassment. I really need to get a better filter. I hadn't meant to say that out loud, but Dylan seemed to like it. He dips his head back down, this time sinking his teeth into my inner thigh, first one, and then the other, before licking away the sting.

"Oh shit…" I breathe out, spreading my legs wider for him.

"You like that? Like when I mark you, baby girl? Like knowing you belong to me and no one else?"

I whimper and nod my head, unable to form words at the moment. I want to be his. I want him as my own, my one and only.

Without warning, Dylan throws one of my legs over his shoulder, and then the other, before flattening his tongue and licking every part of me. My back bows off the ground as I shove more of my dripping, needy cunt into his face. I can't help it. The way his warm, soft tongue laps at my wetness and then circles my clit has me practically fucking his face.

I feel his hands slide under my ass and grip me there, his fingers digging in deeper with each rough stroke of his tongue. He's helping me find my rhythm as I rub my greedy pussy against his mouth.

"D-Dylan, please…" I gasp, clawing at the carpet and snapping my thighs around his head.

He grunts and focuses his attention on my clit, rubbing tight circles around my swollen button with his tongue. I can't stop the breathy moans falling from my lips repeatedly, each one louder than the last as my muscles lock up and my pussy quivers around his tongue.

I teeter on the sharp edge of ecstasy, wanting to savor the aching pressure as it builds. When Dylan scrapes his teeth against my clit, pleasure slices through me, unleashing my pent-up need in one vicious explosion.

I cry out and lift up off the floor, unable to contain the painful bliss rippling through every cell in my body. Wave after wave crashes into me in such rapid succession I don't have time to catch my breath before I'm drawn under once again.

Dylan pushes me back down onto the carpet with one large hand spread out over my belly, making me take all of what he's offering. My skin burns between my thighs where his stubble is scraping me, but it only serves to heighten the pleasure taking over my body.

Finally, fucking *finally*, I start to come back down. I'm a shaking, sweating, puddle of satisfaction. My legs fall from Dylan's shoulders as he gets up on his knees and pulls out his dick.

Holy fucking fuck. I mean, just...

"I'm not fucking you today, princess. But I need this," he grunts, stroking his massive cock. "Daddy needs to come so goddamn hard."

I nod my head and spread my legs open for him, seeing his need and wanting to meet it. Dylan groans and stares at me, jerking himself off to my exposed body. I watch in awe as his massive shaft grows even longer and then swells up. Dylan hisses and throws his head back, pumping his fist furiously.

When he tips his head back down to look at me, his eyes have gone nearly black. He bares his teeth and clenches his jaw before inching closer and pressing the tip of his cock against my clit.

I gasp at how amazing it feels having his hot, hard dick rubbing against me. Dylan lets out a roar as he comes on my pussy, releasing his seed in forceful jets against my clit. An unexpected orgasm rips through me. It's short but so damn intense I see black spots in the corners of my vision.

"That's it, that's so fucking it," Dylan groans as the last of his pleasure fades.

He falls on top of me, catching himself on his forearms so he doesn't crush me completely. His lips are on mine, giving me a taste of my own release, even as I feel his drip down my pussy. When Dylan pulls back, I see his chin glistening with my cum, which makes me lean up and kiss him again.

We finally break apart for air, and a shiver works its way down my spine. Dylan doesn't waste a single second in scooping me up and carrying me through his house, presumably to his bedroom. I don't fight him at all, I just curl up into his arms, resting my head on his shoulder.

Carefully, he sets me down in front of his king-sized bed, then Dylan begins stripping me out of my clothes. He takes his time pressing kisses all over my skin as he peels off my dress, followed by my bra.

"So beautiful," he murmurs, his voice full of awe. It's hard not to believe him when he's looking at me like this. Somehow, this perfect specimen of a man finds me irresistible.

"You're pretty okay, too," I say with a cheeky grin. Dylan darts his eyes up to meet mine, then he freaking winks, which is far more charming than it should be, and gives me a peck on the lips.

I watch as my Daddy tugs off his shirt, revealing his defined chest and rock hard abs to me for the first time. Without thinking about it, I reach out and trail my fingers over his thick muscles, gasping when he tenses and flexes beneath my touch.

"You feel so good, little girl," he groans, tipping his head back. He lets me stroke him a few more times before he gathers up my hands and guides me over to the bed. "Let me hold you tonight. I just want to feel you in my arms."

I nod, because how the heck can I say no to that? Dylan pulls the covers back, motioning for me to get in first. He crawls in behind me, then spoons his body around mine, holding me close while kissing the back of my neck.

Dylan whispers how precious I am and thanks me for trusting him. I blink back tears at his words, loving his praise, but not sure what to do with it. I fall asleep to the rhythm of his heart and the soft, low rumble of his voice. I don't think I've ever been more content in my entire life.

Chapter Seven

Dylan

Something stirs against me, and I slowly pull myself from the blissful dream state I was in. The sweetest smell curls around me as I become more aware of my surroundings. Soft, silky hair brushes against my chest, and I finally open my eyes, taking in the most precious, perfect sight to wake up to.

Sarah is curled against my side, her head resting on my chest while her delicate breaths tickle my skin. I gently comb my fingers through her hair, watching the strands slip through my hand and fall around Sarah's face. Her cheeks are a warm pink from sleep, and I bend down, needing to kiss each one.

My princess blinks her eyes sleepily, then tips her head up, hitting me with those otherworldly eyes. The sweetest smile tugs at her lips, her blush growing deeper the longer I stare at her.

"Morning," I murmur, pressing a kiss to her forehead.

"Morning," she mumbles, burying her face into the side of my neck. I smooth a hand down her back, pressing my little girl closer to me. I'm not sure if she's just tired or if she's suddenly shy around me, but I want to reassure her she can be herself with me and I'll love her just as she is.

Holy shit. Love?

"What has you growling so early in the day?" Sarah asks, lifting her head slightly to throw me the cutest little smirk.

Did I growl? I suppose it's an appropriate reaction to realizing my whole life and all of my priorities are changing right in front of my eyes. I don't think Sarah is ready to hear that though, so I nip at her chin, causing her to laugh.

"I don't growl," I say in a gruff voice, nuzzling into the side of her neck. Sarah squeals and wiggles against me, the feeling of my stubble tickling her sensitive skin.

"You totally growl," she says through laughter. "When someone sneezes in class, or asks a question you just answered, or... walks in *two minutes* late..." God, the look she levels at me has my dick standing at attention. So fucking feisty.

"I see you haven't learned your lesson about that sassy mouth of yours, baby girl," I say with a stern look. Sarah's teal eyes flash, a delightfully wicked smile spreading across her face.

"Maybe if I had a better teacher..."

I roll on top of her, cutting her off with a kiss. She writhes beneath me, her curvy body wiggling against my chest and abs.

"You need another lesson, princess? Need me to show you what else you can do with that mouth?"

Sarah nibbles on her bottom lip, the flush spreading across her cheeks almost enough to make me come on the spot. I've tasted her, teased her, spanked her juicy little ass, and still she blushes so sweetly. God, I'm fucked up for wanting to corrupt her.

"Yes, please," she whispers, looking up at me with clear blue eyes. Sarah blinks, her long lashes brushing against her rosy cheeks. She's so pure, so innocent, so fucking *mine*, I can't think straight.

I flip my beautiful baby girl so she's spread out on top of me, naked and clinging to my shoulders. The surprised giggle that erupts warms me up, reminding me how special, how precious she is.

Sarah pushes herself up, sliding down my body until she's staring at my dick. God, I didn't think I could get any harder, but having her attention, seeing her lust-filled gaze, and Christ, watching her lick her lips...

She deepens her grin and reaches out for me, circling her small, delicate hand over my hard length.

I throw my head back and hiss out a breath.

Fuck. How does this feel so damn good?

The woman has barely touched me and I'm about to go off.

"Oh, did I hurt you?"

I laugh when I open my eyes and see her face painted with worry.

"No, baby girl. You feel so goddamn good. I'm trying not to come yet."

"Oh," she whispers, her cheeks tinted with pink.

"Tighten your hold on me, good, like that," I groan, praising her while trying to keep my shit together. "Faster, baby. Need that mouth of yours too."

Sarah grows more confident, squeezing my thick length and moving her hand up and down my cock. She moves faster now, and I close my eyes to savor this moment. Fuck, if her hand feels this good, I can't wait to be inside her mouth. Her pussy. Her ass.

My princess readjusts herself, kneeling between my legs and taking my dick in both of her hands. Precum dribbles out of the tip and I watch as her eyes grow dark. Sarah bends down and licks it off of me like I'm a goddamn lollipop.

"That's it," I hiss.

She quirks up an eyebrow and grins that little sexy grin again. I don't think I'll ever get tired of seeing her look at me like that. It makes my dick leak, getting more precum all over her hands.

Sarah dips her head down and takes me as far back into her mouth as she can. I feel her gag around me, and it feels fucking fantastic. My hand weaves in her hair as I pull her back a bit.

"Easy, baby girl. Relax. You feel so good," I encourage. "Breathe through your nose and–shit, yes..."

Sarah follows my instruction, then hollows out her cheeks, sucking me hard and fast as her head bobs up and down my cock. I feel her spit dripping down my length, which only makes me harder.

She pops off my dick and stares up at me, biting her lip.

"Am I doing okay, Daddy?"

"Fucking hell, Sarah. You're doing amazing. Love being inside your mouth. You can't do anything wrong here, little girl. I'm all yours."

"Can I...can I lick your, um...?" She points to my balls, which makes them draw up tight.

I groan at her mix of innocence and sex queen.

"Fuck yeah you can," I practically growl, losing myself already to my lust.

I feel her hot little tongue dart out of her mouth and lick my balls. My hips buck at the jolt of pleasure. I can't believe this is really happening. Yeah, I've pictured it countless times in my head over the last few weeks, but this is a hundred times better. A thousand. A million. I'll never get enough.

Sarah sucks my balls into her mouth while fisting my cock. I cry out as she jerks me off and sucks me, the dual sensations pushing me closer to the edge. Then, she switches it up on me, swallowing down my dick while massaging my balls with her hand.

"Such a good girl," I rasp, pleasure shooting down my spine as I shake from head to toe. "I'm not going to last much longer."

I squeeze my eyes shut, trying to hold back what is sure to be a life-changing orgasm. I never want it to end, and yet I want this ache to go away. I want to finally be satisfied, though I have a feeling that won't happen until I'm deep inside of her sweet pussy.

My baby girl moans around me, the vibrations traveling up my dick and hitting me deep inside. She must notice how I'm swelling and throbbing inside of her mouth, because she moans again, swallowing me deeper.

I tug her hair, feeling my orgasm start to tingle in the base of my spine.

"Gonna come," I warn her. "Take it all, princess. Take everything Daddy gives you."

She moans and digs her fingers into my thighs as she shoves herself further down my length, deep throating me as I explode in her mouth.

"Sarah! Fuck!" I roar, my dick twitching, again and again, pumping more of my seed down her hot little throat. She swallows every drop as I keep coming, longer and harder than I ever have.

I must pass out for a second, because when I open my eyes, Sarah is curled up at my side, one arm flung over my torso as she rubs my chest in soothing circles.

"Shit," I manage to breathe out.

She giggles, and I dip my head down to kiss the tip of her nose.

"Did I get a passing grade?" she teases, licking her lips.

"You, little girl, are my star student."

She gives me a sweet smile before pressing a kiss to my lips. It turns from innocent to scorching in a matter of seconds, just like every time we touch. I can feel her restless energy, the tension in her movements, the plea in her kiss for me to give her pleasure in the way only her Daddy can.

"Your turn, princess," I growl, rolling her onto her back and peppering kisses down the curves of her body until I reach her core.

Goddamn, her perfect pink folds are dripping for me, her clit throbbing and begging for my attention. I watch as a drop of her arousal leaks out and drips down her ass. I want to lick it up.

So, I do.

"Dylan!" she cries out, the sound almost painful in how desperate she is for release.

I spear my tongue and tunnel in and out of her tight hole, massaging her walls. Then I flatten my tongue and drag her sweet honey up to her clit, where I circle again and again with my tongue.

When I slip a finger inside of her, she gasps and spasms beneath me. It makes me want to beat my chest with pride that I'm giving her so much pleasure she can hardly contain herself. I work a second finger inside, scissoring them to open her up for me. She tries to buck her hips, but I place my hand on her stomach, spreading my fingers out.

"Let me take care of you, baby girl. Daddy knows what you need."

Sarah's eyes flash, her channel pulsing around my fingers when she hears my title. I didn't know I had this side to me, but with my little girl, it feels right. Others might not understand, but they don't have to. It's between me and Sarah. I pump my fingers in and out of her, curling them up to hit her G-spot. Sarah gasps and bites her lip, her whole body trembling beneath my fingers and tongue.

"Mmm... Daddy, please..."

My cock twitches, growing impossibly harder at hearing that word escape her mouth while she's writhing in pleasure. I work my fingers faster and swirl her clit with my thumb.

"Are you going to come for me, baby girl?"

"Y-y-yes...oh, fuck..."

"Look at me," I demand.

Her eyes snap open as I curl my fingers and press my thumb into her clit. Sarah detonates, thrashing her head as she cries out her pleasure. I hold her body still and continue to lap up everything she's giving me. The final tremors of her explosive orgasm dissipate, leaving Sarah in a satisfied puddle on the bed.

Crawling up her body, I place open-mouthed kisses over every single place I can touch, groaning at her sweet flavor and the way she lifts herself up to meet my lips.

Sarah's eyes are closed, her chest heaving with labored breaths, and she's never been more beautiful than she is right now. I gather her limp body into my arms, cradling her against my chest while her breathing slowly returns to normal.

"You did so good, little girl," I whisper, kissing the top of her head. "So sexy for me, so eager to please." Sarah nods her head and lets out the cutest little sigh. "You're perfect for me, princess."

Sarah finally opens her eyes, those bright teal irises locking onto mine. "You're pretty perfect for me, too."

"Pretty perfect?"

Sarah smiles and rolls her eyes, forcing me to pepper her face with kisses until she giggles and pushes me away. "Fine, you're kind of amazing. And you make me feel..." She trails off, but I cup her face and encourage her to continue. "Seen," she whispers. "And safe. Like everything will be taken care of as long as I'm with you."

I could beat my fucking chest with pride that my little girl feels safe with me. "Good. That's exactly how I want you to feel." I kiss her one last time, then urge her to sit up. "Now, it's Saturday. Let's grab breakfast and then I can take you out."

Sarah grows stiff, turning to look at me over her shoulder. "Is it smart to go out in public together? We could be seen."

I furrow my brow and grunt, not liking the reminder of our precarious situation. No way in hell am I giving my little girl up now that I know how it feels waking up next to her in the morning and falling asleep with her in my arms.

An idea filters in through the morning fog and post-orgasm bliss, and I hop out of bed, ready to get started. "Do you trust me?" I ask when Sarah gives me a questioning look.

"You know I do," she says exasperatedly.

I grin at her response, then grab her hand and pull her out of bed. The sheet falls away from her body, revealing her perfectly curvy body to me. With a concentrated effort, I pull my gaze up to her face.

"Good. Then let me take care of everything while you wash up in the shower."

She opens her mouth to give me more sass, but I cut her off with a quick kiss, then spin her around and give her a light spank, sending her on her way. I can't wait to spend the day with her, and then hopefully, the rest of my life.

Chapter Eight

Sarah

"Where are we going?" I ask, practically bouncing in my seat as Dylan exits off the freeway.

"So impatient," he chides playfully, giving me a wink.

Dylan followed me to my apartment, then waited while I grabbed a change of clothes. We've been on the road for about twenty minutes, and I must have asked him three times already where he's taking me.

"So mysterious," I counter, lifting an eyebrow.

The grin he gives me is devastating to my fresh pair of panties. It's all I can do not to tell him to pull over so I can climb on his lap. Where this wanton side of me came from, I have no idea. Only that I've never felt it with anyone else before.

We ride in comfortable silence until Dylan pulls into a mostly empty parking lot of a nondescript warehouse.

"Uh, is this the part where you chop me up into little pieces and bury my remains in an unfinished construction site before pouring concrete over me?"

A rich, full laugh fills the car, making me warm and tingly from head to toe. "That's quite an imagination you have, princess."

"I didn't hear a no..." Dylan unbuckles his seatbelt, then clicks mine open, nearly pulling me over the console as he kisses me hard and deep.

"No, my sassy girl, I'm not going to chop you up in little pieces," he murmurs against my lips. "The thought of harming one hair on your head makes me physically ill."

An unexpected wave of emotion sweeps through me, and I find myself blinking back tears. I've only known this man for a few weeks, and we've really only connected in the last twenty four hours. How can he already care more about me than my own family?

"Hey," Dylan says, his thumb coming up to brush a stray tear from my cheek. "What are you thinking about? Did I say something wrong?"

"No," I insist, shaking my head. "The opposite. You're... you're too good to be true, you know? I still don't know what you see in me, and when you say things like that, I get all kinds of crazy ideas." I didn't mean to say all of that, but Dylan has a way of bringing out all of my secret thoughts, apparently.

"Crazy ideas like what?"

"Nothing. Never mind."

He looks like he wants to press me on the issue, but decides against it. Smart man. I can't even imagine what he'd say if I told him I wanted to spend the rest of my life with him after such a short time together. That's impossible, anyway, so there's no use getting my hopes up. I wouldn't ask him to give up his job and put a blemish on his career just to be with me.

"Come on, let's go inside," Dylan says with a smile. "Take your mind off of whatever has you doubting me."

"I'm not..." He gives me a look that warns me not to bullshit him. I shut my mouth and hop out of the car, hoping to avoid his all-knowing gaze for a few seconds.

Dylan takes my hand, lacing our fingers together as we walk up to a back entrance. I'm a little nervous, but mostly I'm just thrilled to be with him. I'd walk around a garbage dump as long as Dylan was by my side, squeezing my hand like he is now.

The door swings open as we get closer, and an older gentleman ushers us inside. "Dylan Cole!" the man greets. Dylan nods his head. "Good to see you again. I'll be in the back working on payroll and paperwork if you need anything. Thanks again for your business today. I appreciate being able to get caught up on work and not have to lose money by shutting the place down." Dylan shakes the man's hand and then we watch him scurry off to the back room.

"What was that about? And where the heck are we?" I ask, bouncing on the balls of my feet.

"You're a nursing student, correct?"

"Yes..." I answer suspiciously. "If this is about checking someone's mole or something, I just want to remind you I'm not official yet."

Dylan chuckles and rests a hand on the small of my back, leading me further into the dimly lit building. We turn a corner and Dylan flips a switch, illuminating the huge space.

I gasp and cover my mouth with my hands, stepping forward to look at every single thing on display. "What is this place?" I whisper, my eyes darting around like a ping pong ball.

"A little-known medical curiosity museum," he says, stepping up behind me. Dylan rests his hands on my hips, pulling me against him as he leans down and presses a kiss to my temple. "I met the owner, Craig, at a convention hosted by the university several years ago. He's curated some of the weirdest stuff, and I thought you might enjoy it. I rented out the place today, so it's all ours."

"Really?" I whisper, turning to look at him over my shoulder. That must have been what Craig was talking about earlier, before he made himself scarce.

"Really," Dylan confirms. "Do you like it?"

His golden eyes shine with a hint of vulnerability as they search mine. I still can't believe he wants to impress me, but he accomplished his mission nonetheless.

"It's incredible," I tell him honestly. "Holy crap, is that a shrunken head?" I point to a row of clear containers with floating heads inside. To most people, it might be gross, but I find these things fascinating. Before Dylan gets a chance to answer, I'm taking off in that direction. I get side tracked by another display, though. "It's a brain!"

Dylan chuckles as he steps up beside me. He doesn't say anything, he just smiles down at me as if I'm the most precious thing in the world. I beam under his attention, then focus on the brain that's sliced in half in front of me. It shouldn't be romantic, but the fact that he thought about me and went through the effort to make this happen has me heating up from the inside out.

We walk around to the different displays, and Dylan asks me questions when I linger on certain ones. I don't always have an answer, but when I do, he hangs on my every word before telling me how smart or clever I am. My own parents have never paid this much attention to me, let alone took an interest in my life. And when Dylan praises me? God, it probably shouldn't turn me on or please me this much, but I crave more of his words, his touch, his everything.

"Why did you want to become a nurse?" he asks as we make a second loop around the room to make sure we didn't miss anything.

"At first, it was because I knew my father would disapprove," I admit with a smirk. Dylan laughs softly, encouraging me to continue. "But the more I thought about it, the more it felt right. My parents weren't very subtle with the fact that they wanted a boy instead of a girl. Due to complications with my mom's pregnancy, she wasn't able to have any more children, which they also blame me for."

"Fuck them," Dylan grits out. I stop walking and wrap my arms around my Daddy, loving that he's automatically taking my side. He runs his fingers through my hair, something he seems to love, and I melt into his embrace.

"I just want to do something real with my life. Something that matters. My parents want me to become some trophy wife to further their political and financial goals, but I want to be... I don't know. Important. I can do so much more than play the part I've been groomed to play my whole life, and nursing feels like a way to break those bonds completely, you know?"

I tip my head back, looking into those amber eyes full of awe and understanding. "You're so strong," he murmurs, kissing my forehead. More of his sweet words fill my heart, and I know I'll treasure each one of them.

"The more I studied the science and chemistry behind nursing, the more fascinated I became. I thought briefly about becoming a doctor, but ultimately stuck with nursing. The combination of medical knowledge and care-giving felt like the perfect fit. I just want to help people, you know? Maybe even erase some of the horrible ways my parents have treated others in the past."

"Princess," Dylan says softly, cupping my chin. "I don't even know where to start. Your big heart is admirable, and your work ethic is impressive. But I don't want you thinking, not for one second, that you have to balance some karmic scale because of your parents. Their actions are their own."

"I know," I sigh, turning my head so Dylan drops his hold on my chin. I look down at the floor, then let out another breath. I feel raw and vulnerable, exposing everything I've held close to my heart for so long. "I just... I want to matter to someone. I want to make a difference."

"Sarah," Dylan whispers. "Look at me." I do as he says, unable to disobey him. "I love your compassion and drive, but I need you to know you already mean the world to someone."

"Oh?" I'm barely holding back a smile, as well as tears. This man has me feeling all sorts of things, and I want to dive in head first, ready for more.

"Me," he answers, kissing my cheeks and nose. "You're Daddy's precious little girl. I'm so proud of you."

"You are?" This time, I can't stop the tears.

"Always," he confirms, wrapping me up in his arms again. Dylan holds me for long moments, rocking me gently back and forth.

Eventually, we untangle ourselves and Dylan leads me back to his car with a hand on the small of my back. I love that he can't seem to stop touching me. The entire time we were in the museum, he was holding my hand or playing with my hair. Anything to keep our connection going.

Dylan takes off toward his home, though I'm not sure if it's just so I can get my car and leave or if he's going to ask me to stay the night again. I don't want to go back to my cold, empty apartment. I want to stay with my Daddy as long as he'll have me.

We pull into the driveway and he cuts the engine, resting his hands on the steering wheel. I watch them flex, his knuckles turning white before Dylan exhales forcefully.

What is he thinking? Oh, God, is he waiting for me to get out and go back to my car? Does he regret everything that's happened between us? Has he finally realized I'm not worth risking his career over? Of course, he's snapped out of our little fantasy world.

My fingers twitch, and I look out the passenger side window before staring down at my hands. Taking a shaky breath, I manage to lift my hand to the door handle, and pull. Hard. I need out of here before my brain has a chance to catch up with my broken heart.

I lunge out of the vehicle, only to be pulled back by my seatbelt. Dammit, how embarrassing can I be right now?

"Sarah–"

"I got it," I choke out, scrambling to unbuckle myself so I can jump in my own car and drive off the nearest bridge.

"Sarah," Dylan says again, his hands surrounding mine, stopping my frantic movements. "Tell me what you're thinking about."

I can't look him in the eye, so I stare at the floorboard, willing it to open up so I can slip through it.

"I was just going to get out of your hair," I say, trying to sound casual and unaffected.

"What? Why?" Dylan growls. I wince at his harsh tone, and he curses softly under his breath. "I didn't mean to scare you," he says more calmly. "The thought of you leaving me..." He squeezes my hands, then lifts one up, pressing a kiss to the inside of my wrist. "Tell me what's *really* going on in your head, princess. The truth this time."

I shrug, but Dylan isn't having any of that. He cups my chin, gently but with a firm grip, forcing my eyes to meet his. "I thought maybe you were done with me," I whisper, hating how desperate and pathetic I sound. "You were just sitting there and you seemed upset, and I know everything is complicated, and–"

He tugs me forward, crashing his lips against mine in an all-consuming kiss. Every doubt falls away as his tongue invades my mouth, stroking in deep as he breathes me in. My hands claw at his shirt as I fist the material, wanting him closer, closer, closer.

Dylan groans, tangling his fingers in my hair and pulling my head back so he can devour my neck. I pant and whimper as he nips my skin and licks away the sting.

"Not done with you," he grunts as he makes his way back up to my mouth. "Never done with you," he murmurs right before kissing the air from my lungs.

I eventually push him away so I can suck down air, and Dylan makes a pained sound, like it hurts being this far away. "You seemed so angry..." I trail off, still catching my breath.

"I was trying not to haul you over my shoulder and toss you down on my bed before tearing your tight, virgin pussy in two," he grits out.

"Oh." That thought literally never occurred to me. He was trying to restrain himself? Because his lust is too much? "That's like... really fucking hot," I mumble, still a little light headed from his kisses.

Dylan groans, then tucks my hair behind my ear and nuzzles into the side of my neck. "I won't ever take advantage of you," he whispers.

"What if I want you to?" I look up at Dylan, his golden eyes glowing and jaw tense. He looks feral, and I love it. Dylan's nostrils flare as he takes labored breaths, and I swear he's trembling as he continues to stare at me.

I sway toward him, wanting his mouth on mine once more, but Dylan leaps out of the car, slides across the hood, and rips my door open. One second I'm gaping up at my professor, and the next second I'm lifted from the car and flung over his shoulder.

"Dylan!" I squeal. He clamps his arm over my thighs, keeping me secure, while his other hand spanks me twice.

"Told you I wasn't done with you," he growls, making me laugh.

Dylan hauls me inside, then straight back to where his room is. He kicks the door shut, then I'm flying through the air briefly, before my back hits the mattress. I'm smiling up at my Daddy, breathless and so very turned on.

"Christ, little girl. What you do to me..."

He falls on top of me, catching himself with his forearms at the last second. I spread my legs for him, cradling his hips as I open my mouth and welcome his kiss. We get lost in each other, touching, grabbing, pawing at each other to get more, more, more.

Something tears, and I'm vaguely aware of my dress being tossed aside, followed by my bra and panties. I don't know how he managed to get me and himself naked with absolutely zero help from me, but I don't care. I press myself against his thick, muscled body, grinding my bare pussy against his leg that's thrust between my thighs.

"Sarah," he groans, turning me so I'm on my back. "Need to lick up your little cunt before I claim you."

"Mmhm," I readily agree, my head spinning from lust and euphoria.

Dylan slides off the bed, kneeling on the floor in front of me. I don't get a chance to take a breath before he pins my legs to the bed and drives his face deep into my soaking wet pussy. I cry out when he spears his tongue into my entrance, his nose circling my clit. The man is suffocating on me, but he doesn't seem to mind. In fact, he seems possessed, addicted, wild with the need to have more of me. All of me.

I grip his hair and hold on while Dylan eats me out with such intensity, I start grinding into him and panting his name over and over again. My muscles tense, my spine bows off the bed, and my head falls back as I give myself over completely to him.

My abs are so tight they burn, and my thighs are trembling. My orgasm is right there, more forceful and urgent than anything I've ever felt before. He hums into my quivering pussy and gives his head a shake. I cry out, a sharp, jagged sound, and fall over the edge. The fire in my belly expands, spreading through my limbs and up into my cheeks. It settles in my ears, making the whole world muffled and fuzzy. By the time it recedes into a warm glow, he's kneading my thighs and kissing my belly.

"Delicious." I feel more than hear him, his voice rumbling over my skin as he continues placing open-mouthed kisses over my breasts and collarbone, making his way slowly up my neck and then finally crashing his lips down on mine in a possessive, punishing kiss. I taste myself on him, but I can't get enough. I kiss him back with the same passion he's giving me, moaning into his mouth and biting his bottom lip.

He growls and dives back in, sucking the air out of my lungs and replacing it with pure, raw lust. I need him. Fucking *crave* him. I feel inexplicably empty without his thick cock filling me up. I open my legs wider for him as he settles his hips into me and grinds his shaft against my folds, not yet entering me.

"Are you sure?" he grits out. I can tell he's on edge, and while I appreciate his restraint, that's not what I want. I want that animalistic side of him again. I want to feel his power, his strength as he moves inside of me.

"Please, Daddy," I whisper.

"Be careful, little girl," he warns. "I'm on the edge, and I don't know if I can go slow."

"I don't want slow," I insist. "I just want to feel you."

"You don't know what you're asking for," Dylan groans as he drags his thickness through my folds, the hot, hard head of his cock scraping against my clit in shallow thrusts. "I'm going to tear you apart unless you tell me to stop."

I cup the sides of his face, urging the big, beastly professor to open his eyes and look at me. I'm blown away by the raw need swimming in his golden irises, along with something more tender. I know my Daddy would never hurt me. I trust him to bring us both pleasure while keeping me safe.

"I want this," I murmur, nodding my head as I wiggle my hips. "I want you." He opens his mouth to protest, but I cover it with my hand. Dylan looks so stunned I almost let out a laugh. I think I like surprising him like this. "Please fuck me now, Daddy." His eyes glow, turning from golden brown to molten lava at my words. I swear I feel his gaze burn into every inch of me as sweat beads against my temples.

"Jesus, you're perfect, little girl. And mine. All fucking *mine*," he roars as he slams into me in one earth-shattering thrust. I swear he just ripped me in half. And I want more. So much more.

"Yes, yes…" I yell over and over as he sets a relentless pace.

"I can't stop," he chokes out. "I'm sorry, princess, I can't… holy shit," he grunts as he thrusts in and out of me, stuffing me full of his dick and filling me full to bursting.

I claw at his back, already starting to lose control. "Don't stop," I whimper. I shake and tense and prepare for the onslaught of sensations to overpower me completely. "More," I beg, clinging to him and meeting him thrust for thrust.

In one swift move, Dylan flips us so I'm on top of him. I gasp and then moan as he grips my hips and slowly, so slowly guides my body down his long, thick shaft.

"That's it, ride me, my dirty little princess. Take what you need from me."

I steady myself by placing my hands on his chest, and then I test out what feels good. He gives me the confidence to own my pleasure and sexuality, to do as he says, and take what I need. Dylan looks only too happy to give me whatever I want.

I grind down on him, which makes us both groan. Getting up on my knees, I swivel my hips, massaging the very tip of his dick with my already throbbing channel. I love the way his pupils dilate and his jaw flexes. I love the power I have over him in this moment.

Without warning, I drop down on him, allowing his hard cock to pierce me through and through. It's a sharp, exquisite feeling to have him inside of me like this. I whimper when I feel him bump up against my cervix.

"Goddamn, Sarah, holy fuck, baby, you feel so good, so good..."

Hearing his praise and watching his face tense as he holds on to his control has me spiraling towards the edge. I glide up and down his shaft, riding him nice and hard until I'm a quivering mess, gushing all over him and moaning uncontrollably. I lean forward, placing a hand on either side of his head and grinding down on him, rocking back and forth, sliding my clit over the base of his cock again and again.

Dylan bites my nipples and sucks on my breasts, heightening my pleasure with each swipe of his tongue. I feel his large hands grip my hips to hold me in place while he fucks up into me with long, rough strokes.

My orgasm slams into me, wringing out my bones and stealing my strength. I collapse on top of him, my pussy snapping around him again and again.

Dylan doesn't even give me a chance to breathe before he rolls me onto my back and throws my legs over his shoulders. I somehow need him all over again, even though I haven't fully come down from my last release. He must see the uncontainable desire in my eyes as he rubs his hard, swollen dick up and down my slit.

Again and again he teases me, builds me up, never quite giving me what I need.

And then he fucks me, hitting me so damn deep, stretching me and filling me and punishing me as he spears his cock in and out of my cunt, fucking me into a frenzy. I scream his name and he shouts mine. We're wild, unhinged, rabid with lust and love.

I arch my back and feel him sliding deeper inside of me. I lose it completely, my mind whirling and spinning in patterns of pleasure and heaven, lost entirely in the physical act of fucking, lost entirely in the bliss that's closing in around me. I come again, my release wrecking me completely. I come hard and long, the orgasm ripping my core to pieces. I'm gasping and straining as it rolls over me like a wave.

I'm vaguely aware of Dylan's cock pulsing inside of me and filling me up with his warm, sticky seed, but my vision blurs and darkens around the edges.

When I come to, Dylan has me draped over his chest. He's rubbing my back in calming circles, handling me with such tender care. "Breathe, baby girl. Breathe for me," he whispers.

I do as he says, the oxygen filling my lungs and sending an unexpected tremor through my limbs. Dylan groans and tips my head up, kissing me slow and deep. When we break apart, he tucks my hair behind my ear and cradles my face in his hand, rubbing his thumb over my jaw. He looks at me with such devotion, such awe.

I smile shyly at him. Somehow his penetrating gaze feels so much more vulnerable that the mind-blowing sex we just had.

"I won't ever get enough of you, princess. Your body, your mind, your fucking soul. I want it all," he says so softly, so reverently.

"It's yours, Daddy," I tell him truthfully.

He kisses me again, letting it linger as he presses me even closer to him. We stay like that, foreheads touching, lips inches apart, limbs tangled up, for what feels like hours. I never want to leave his side, but I know things are complicated. For now though, I'm content to soak up every second of being with this incredible man.

Chapter Nine

Dylan

Warm, golden light peeks through the curtains, spilling out onto the bed and making Sarah's skin glow everywhere it touches. Her gorgeous, silky black hair glitters in the sunlight, only adding to the ethereal effect. It's just past nine in the morning and I know she needs more sleep, but I need to taste her. I can't get enough of her sweet scent. I'm fucking addicted to tasting her as she creams around my tongue. Something tells me she won't mind my morning wakeup call.

I turn toward her, smiling when Sarah sighs in her sleep and rolls onto her back. Perfect. Just how I want her. I kiss her rosy cheeks and trail my lips down her neck while sliding my hands up her naked body. Sarah shivers beneath my touch but doesn't wake up. Her smooth, porcelain skin contrasts with her dusky pink nipples, which are hard little peaks, begging for my teeth and tongue.

Without wasting another second, I lean down and suck on her breast, teasing her with little bites and soft licks. Sarah moans softly and bows her back, offering herself up to me, even in her sleep.

I switch to her other breast, giving it the same attention. I can feel her heart pounding in her chest. I swear I smell her getting wet for me. The thought makes me groan as my hand comes up to play with her other nipple. Each swipe of my tongue elicits a breathy moan, making my dick ache and leak precum.

"Dylan?" Sarah's confused, sexy little voice fills the room. She whimpers for me as I pinch one nipple and bite down on the other. "*Yes*! Oh God, yes..."

I look up at her, grunting with satisfaction when I see her eyes closed and her face scrunched up in pure pleasure. Sarah's lips part as she sucks down air. She rocks her hips, rubbing her wet heat against me. I don't think she's even aware she's doing it.

"You like when I play with your tits, princess?"

"Mmhm," she moans, finally opening her eyes. I have to bite the inside of my cheek to keep from coming in my damn pants. Her eyes are deep and dark, glazed over with lust. She licks her lips and winds her fingers through my hair, pulling me up toward her. "I think I'll like anything you do to me," she whispers before sealing her lips over mine.

Sarah dominates this kiss, taking what she needs from me. Her tongue tangles with mine as I swallow down her passion and greedy little moans. She pulls back, gasping for air. I nuzzle into the side of her neck, breathing her in. I can't help but lick her skin, wanting her taste on my tongue.

"Yes, Daddy," Sarah breathes out. "I...need you. Please?"

"Need me to do what, baby girl?" I trail kisses down her neck before sucking on the sensitive spot beneath her ear.

"I-I ache for you. I feel so empty."

I growl and lunge for her, pinning her down to the mattress and devouring her sweet, filthy mouth. "Jesus, woman," I grunt before kissing her again. Sarah wiggles beneath me and spreads her legs wide, letting me settle between them. My heavy cock glides through her folds, making us both groan.

I cup the side of her face and kiss her as I surge forward, groaning when I feel her tight little channel stretch around me. I pull out, grunting when her pussy clamps down, trying to suck me back in.

"More," Sarah whispers, wrapping her legs around my hips. "Deeper. I want it all."

"How do good girls ask?" I growl, nipping at her lips.

"Please!" she whines, rocking her hips frantically. "I need it, Daddy. Please."

"Fuck," I growl, pulling out and then slamming my dick back inside her greedy little cunt. She feels so damn good, so tight and wet for me. Sarah inhales sharply and then exhales a breathy moan.

Her pussy ripples around me, sucking me in deeper, deeper, so fucking deep I see stars behind my eyes. I grit my teeth, hanging on to my orgasm by a thread. Sarah clings to me as I rock in and out of her. My thrusts become more forceful, and my needy girl loves it. She plants her feet on the bed and lifts her hips, meeting me brutal thrust for brutal thrust.

I scrape my cock along her front wall, searching for that one spot...

"Fuck!" Sarah cries out as she spasms around me, her muscles flexing and releasing, squeezing my dick so damn tight as she comes around me like a goddess.

I fucking snap.

I hammer into her, hitting her G-spot over and over, grunting as I fuck her right through her first orgasm and into another one. Sarah screams out my name and claws at my back, tearing up my skin. It hurts so damn good.

"Again," I growl, burying my head into the side of her neck. I know I should slow down, but the way my woman is moaning and writhing beneath me, I don't think she minds.

My spine tingles with the first signs of my orgasm. My muscles flex and tense as I try to shove it back down. I'm not ready for this to end yet. White hot bliss courses through me, but I need her to come again before I give up the fight.

I sit back on my heels and pull her legs up to rest them against my chest, changing up the angle. Her already tight pussy squeezes my cock like a vise, pulling a growl from somewhere deep in my chest as I thrust harder, faster, deeper inside her. Sarah's glazed over eyes roll to the back of her head and her mouth hangs open, rewarding my rough strokes with greedy little whimpers as I bring us closer and closer to our climax.

"Oh God, I think I'm..."

"Yes baby girl, that's right. Come for me. I want to feel you come all over Daddy's hard fucking cock."

Her body responds to me immediately, that sweet pussy massaging me as I lean in for another kiss. She arches her back and I know she's close. Just a little more. Fuck, I'm going to come, but I need her to get there first.

"Yes," she whispers. "Yes, yes, yes…"

"Who does this pussy belong to?" I snarl, unable to hold back the beast inside me.

"You," she cries out.

"Say my fucking name, angel. Say my name when you come for me."

"Daddy! Ohmygod, yes, I'm coming so hard, Daddy…"

I feel her climax as it rushes through her, overwhelming her curvy little body as she clamps down on my thick dick over and over. I pound into her spasming cunt, losing a little more of myself with each rough stroke until I'm nothing more than a wild animal rutting inside my mate.

Sarah tenses for a heartbeat, then she claws my chest as a raw scream is ripped from her throat. I roar her name as we shatter together, our old selves breaking apart, making way for the new life we're going to build together.

I reluctantly pull out of my woman and collapse beside her, draping her limp, sweaty body over mine. I can feel her heart slamming against her chest as she gasps for air. I rub Sarah's back in calming circles, letting her know she's safe with me, even in this vulnerable state.

My beautiful baby girl finally looks up at me, her blue eyes filled with satisfaction and awe. Yeah, I'm definitely going to need to put that look on her face every chance I get.

"Holy shit," she finally says, making me chuckle.

I tuck some of her hair behind her ear, drawing her up for a kiss. "My thought exactly, princess," I whisper before pressing my lips against her forehead and breathing her in. Sarah hums contentedly and snuggles closer to me. I tuck her head under my chin and continue to rub her back.

"What made you want to study philosophy?" Sarah asks, her voice smooth and content as she idly traces her fingers over my bare skin.

I'm not sure how to respond. I don't share much of myself with anyone, especially about my past. Still, I can't leave her hanging. My sweet girl opened up her heart for me yesterday, let me see her kind spirit and her brokenness. "It captured my attention from a pretty young age," I hedge.

Sarah props herself up on my chest and narrows her sparkling teal eyes at me. "You're being rather dodgy, Professor," she says with a smirk. "If I were to give you an answer like that, you'd spank me, wouldn't you? Is turnabout fair play?"

Before she gets a chance to follow through on that thought, I tickle her sides, laughing when she collapses into a fit of giggles. Jesus, she's so pure, so fucking soft and sweet. I need her light in my life, no matter the consequences. Even if it means baring my scars to the most precious person in the world to me.

Once I get her settled back down in bed beside me, I press a kiss to the top of her head, breathing in her warm, sugary scent. "Books were an escape for me," I finally whisper. "I didn't care whether it was an encyclopedia, a mystery novel, an autobiography, or even a raunchy romance book, as long as it could distract me from my father's mood swings."

Sarah stiffens next to me, and I worry I shared too much. But then, like the sweet girl she is, Sarah presses a kiss right over my heart, then rests her hand there, as if locking it in place. She keeps her hand over my heart as she snuggles down next to me. Crazy as it seems, her simple gesture is healing me more and more with each passing second.

After a few moments of silence, I continue. "I snuck books from the local library, since I didn't understand they were free if I just had a card. My dad never explained any of that to me, and he didn't much approve of my nose in a book. Still, I took whatever I could carry and hid them in my fort on the far south end of the ranch. When my old man started drinking, I knew where I could go to escape."

"A safe haven," Sarah whispers, echoing what I told her earlier.

"Yes," I confirm, kissing her forehead. "A safe haven. I became infatuated with learning and gathering information, which then grew into a curiosity for how we know what we know. And why. What are the rules that govern knowledge and morality? Who put them there? How can we expand on our understanding of them?" I take a breath, relaxing into this moment with my little girl. "My best friend and I had similar difficult childhoods, and we both used education and college as our ticket out. We both ended up moving to New York and graduating college a few years later. Fast forward several more years, and I'm a professor, while my friend, Reed, is the dean of the university."

"Wait, Dean Landis is your bestie?!" Sarah asks, excitement and happiness pouring from her eyes.

"I don't think I've ever called him my *bestie*, but yes, I guess you could say that."

"Oh my gosh, that's so sweet. I mean, I'm sorry your dad was the worst. And I'm sorry Reed's parents weren't any better. But how cool is it that you're still friends? I'm glad you've had someone there for you throughout your life."

Well, damn if my heart didn't just break in half for my little girl. She's never had anyone there for her, yet she has the most tender heart, and is genuinely happy for the friend I've found.

"You have someone now, too," I remind her, smoothing her hair back so I can kiss her cheeks.

"For how long?" I lean back a bit, taking in her wide eyes and furrowed brow. "I'm sorry. I shouldn't have brought it up."

"Sarah," I say sternly, needing her attention. "What we have is..." I exhale, rolling on my back and taking Sarah with me, flinging her over my chest. "It's permanent." My little girl huffs out a breath, and I look down at her, knowing she doesn't believe me. I don't blame her. The connection between us is intense, overwhelming, and like nothing I've ever experienced. Now that I know it exists, though, I can't survive without it. "Just give it time, princess. Let me show you what forever looks like."

"Forever?" God, her tentative whisper guts me, but I just nod and tuck her head under my chin, holding my princess and rocking her back and forth.

"Do you trust me?"

"Yes, Daddy."

"Good girl," I murmur, loving the way she shivers at my praise. I don't know how the hell I'm going to navigate this relationship, only that my sole purpose is to love and cherish my little girl, come whatever may.

Chapter Ten

I drop my backpack on the floor, next to the couch, and plop down, exhaling a deep breath. I just got home from my last class of the day, which means it's officially the weekend. Thank God.

After spending all of last weekend with Dylan, these last five days have been miserable. I've seen him in class, of course, but that's only made things worse. All I want to do is curl up in his lap and tell him about my day while he combs his fingers through my hair. Okay, that, and I want to climb him like a damn tree and beg him to make me come until I can't breathe. He's pretty good at it, too.

Instead, I've had to sit in class, knowing what his hands feel like on my skin, knowing how his amber eyes turn dark when he's thrusting deep inside me, and yet knowing I can't do a damn thing about it.

For his part, Professor Cole had a little more control over his reaction to me, which makes sense. He's a professional. This is his career on the line. No one cares if an undergrad is mooning over him from the front row. In fact, I'm sure there are at least two dozen other students giving Professor Cole the same heated looks in my class alone. Still, I was hoping for maybe a little sign that he's in as much agony as I am.

We decided to wait until this weekend to spend more time together. I get it. Really, I do. We both have work and class, and we can't seem to keep our hands off each other when we're in the same room, so there need to be boundaries.

I keep reminding myself of that, though the rock sitting in the bottom of my gut hasn't moved since I left Dylan's house early Monday morning before class. We've texted throughout the week, but it's not the same. It's like I'm only getting bits and pieces of the professor, but I want all of him. I experienced it over the weekend, and now nothing else will do. But, I guess that will have to wait until I graduate.

My stomach twists again, and I groan, standing up from the couch to head to the kitchen. I don't want to think about going months with only seeing Dylan on the weekends. As I fill up a glass of water, the terrible thought that's been in the back of my mind surfaces.

What if he finally figured out I'm not worth it?

I take a gulp of water, hoping to swallow down the bitter taste. Dylan told me to trust him. He said we were forever. Then again, he said those things after we both had life-altering orgasms, so I'm not sure if it counts. I've been having that debate in my head all week, and it's only compounded by the fact that Dylan hasn't contacted me yet today.

We didn't have set plans or anything, but I thought... Well, I guess I thought he craved me as much as I crave him. I thought he'd want to spend every second with me he possibly could, but so far, I have zero plans for the night.

As I'm loading up the dishwasher with the dishes left from last night, the intercom next to the private elevator buzzes. I hardly ever get guests, but maybe Dylan wanted to surprise me?

Excitement blooms in my lower belly, and I instinctively smooth my shirt down and gather my hair up, twisting it over my shoulder. Taking a deep breath, I try to turn down my smile from full cheesiness to only half cheese. I don't want to come across as too desperate.

The intercom buzzes again, and I practically skip over to it, hitting the button to talk to Dylan.

"Hey!"

"Sarah."

Oh, shit. It's not Dylan. It's my father.

"Come on up," I say, trying to maintain my demeanor. Crap, crap, crap. What does he want? I really don't want to deal with my father right now.

A few moments later, the elevator whines, then the doors open with a ding. My dad strides inside like he owns the place, which, technically, he does. Still, my father seems to think I don't deserve privacy or respect as long as he's footing the bill.

"What have you got on? Is that what you wear to your classes?" he asks, giving me a disapproving glare.

I look down at my light blue sweater, black jeans, and ankle booties. I thought I looked pretty cute. Casual, but still put together.

"Yeah, I found it hard to sit in the desks in class wearing a sequined bodycon dress," I say sarcastically. I hate when he barges in like this, judging everything about my life.

"Maybe if you lost a few pounds..." he mutters, trailing off. It's his go-to insult, but I'd be lying if I said it still didn't sting every time he said it.

"This has been a lovely chat, Dad. Is there anything else you wanted to discuss? Perhaps my lack of designer textbook covers? You know, I don't have any diamonds or fine gems encrusted on my phone case, maybe we could chat about that?"

My father turns on his heel, his face flushed and eyes bulging. I take a step back, then two more as he advances. "You're a real piece of work, Sarah," he spits out.

I stumble over the area rug in my living room, then catch myself on the side of the couch. I've never seen my father this angry, and honestly, he's scaring the shit out of me. "I didn't mean–"

"Shut up!" he roars, wrapping his meaty fist around my forearm. He yanks me forward, then drags me roughly through the apartment to my room. My father pushes me inside, then drops his hold as he tears through my closet.

I rub my arm gently, soothing over the angry red marks left by his fingers. I shuffle backward, leaning against the wall and trying to make myself as small as possible. I've seen my dad upset, and I've been on the receiving end of many a rant, but this is something else entirely.

I watch as he digs through shoes and tosses dresses out left and right. "C-can I help you find something?" I ask tentatively.

The commotion stops, and my dad turns to face me once again. Big mistake. His ruddy face is nearly purple, the vein in his forehead throbbing as he sneers at me. I've never seen him be so ugly, inside and out. "No, you've done quite enough. I shouldn't have left you on your own so much. You insisted on this freedom in college, but I knew you were a rotten apple. I shouldn't have trusted you."

My heart stutters in my chest and I feel nauseous, but I have to know. "What are you talking about? What did I do?"

My dad barks out a laugh, then continues pilfering my closet. A few moments later, he returns with a dark blue dress. This one is floor length, which is surprising, but then I notice the slit running nearly up to the left hip. In my father's other hand are black, six inch Louboutins that I've never worn because... well, six inch Louboutins.

"It doesn't matter now what you did, only what you're going to do moving forward. Show up at Fogo de Chão Tuesday night, wearing this outfit. I'll send Betty over to do your hair and makeup. Sarah, you need to make a good impression. Ralph Edmond has agreed to consider your hand in marriage, despite your... flaws."

My mouth falls open as a million thoughts race through my brain. Anger, injustice, and fear wash over me in waves, each one dragging me further out into a black sea of despair.

"Marriage?" I squeak out. "I c-can't. I won't." I cross my arms over my chest as if that will somehow protect me. My heart feels like it's about to beat right out of my ribcage as tears clog my throat.

"Won't? *Won't?*" my father sneers. "You lost the privilege of making your own choices when you fell into bed with your professor." I gasp, the first tears falling down my cheeks. "Did you think I wouldn't notice? That I didn't have eyes on you? I can't believe, after all your mother and I have done for you, the life and wealth we've provided, you went and... and... turned into a slut."

"Excuse me?!" I say with more force than I thought I was capable of. "You dress me up in skimpy clothes and parade me around! You literally told me to go flirt with some assholes so that you could buddy up to their father about a campaign donation. Are you serious right now?"

The clothes and shoes drop to the floor with a thud as my father takes three measured steps toward me. I try backing up, but I'm already cornered against the wall. He leans down, bringing his face just inches from mine. Fury rolls off his body, every muscle tense as if he's ready for a fight.

"Sleeping your way to a good grade is trashy and far beneath our family."

"But sleeping my way into the right social circles is fine?"

The slap comes out of nowhere, and I'm so shocked, I don't even make a noise. The side of my face stings, though I'm more hurt that my father laid a hand on me. He grabs my chin and snags my head to one side, then the other. "There won't be a mark," he says with a satisfied huff. "But say that shit again and I might not be so generous."

"Why are you doing this?" I manage to whisper.

"The real question is why I haven't done it sooner. Why did I let you run off to college to get an education you'll never use? I suppose I have a soft spot for my only offspring." I resist the urge to roll my eyes, knowing nothing good can come from it. "But the game is over. Let me spell it out for you, *dear daughter.* You will go to dinner Tuesday night. You will do whatever the fuck it takes to secure a marriage proposal. If you're successful, I won't have your precious professor tossed out of the university and all of academia. Have I made myself clear?"

"This isn't his fault. Please don't take this out on Professor Cole," I protest, though I can hear the pleading tone in my voice. I sound weak, and my father knows it.

"Do I look like I care? No. You are *my* daughter, and I didn't raise you just to run off and cause a scandal during re-election year. I'm giving you a choice after all, it seems. Follow through on your date and proposal with Ralph, and save your professor. Or, disobey me and watch me ruin any chance he has at finding a job outside of fast food chains and outlet malls."

"No, no please don't do this," I sob, unable to hold back my emotions any longer. "He doesn't deserve any of that. Please, just... don't do this."

The look my father gives me sends chills down my spine. His normally blue eyes turn black, his nostrils flare, and his jaw trembles with how hard he's clenching his teeth. "The choice is yours," he finally grits out. He slams his fist on the wall next to my head, making me scream and fall to the floor, curling myself into the fetal position.

I stay huddled on the floor for what feels like hours. I listened to my father leave, grumbling the whole way about how ungrateful I am and not worth the headache. His words bounced off of me, and still I stayed on the ground.

When my back starts hurting, I finally uncurl myself, wincing as I stretch out my sore muscles. I try standing up, only to have my knees wobble, sending me tumbling back down. My head is spinning, everything aches, and despite having no tears left, I choke out a pitiful sob. I crawl over to the couch, hauling myself up and hiding under a blanket.

I knew things with Dylan couldn't last forever, despite his promise to me. I just had no idea they would end so soon, and so horribly. I debate calling Dylan, but then my father's words come back to me. He's been watching me. Or, at least, he's paid other people to watch me. Have they tapped my phone? Would they know I reached out?

In the end, I turn my phone on silent and put it on the coffee table. Tucking the blanket over my head, I fall into an uneasy sleep. Maybe when I wake up, this will all be a dream.

Chapter Eleven

Dylan

I rush through the hallways of the university to get to class, nearly knocking over a few students in the process. I never thought I'd be desperate to get to the giant lecture hall where Philosophy 101 is held, but I need to see my princess. Class doesn't start for another thirty minutes, but I'm hoping Sarah is early today. I haven't seen her in days, and I'm desperate for another hit of my favorite drug.

I was held up on Friday, thanks to a student utilizing my office hours. I know it's my job to answer questions and help guide young students, but Heath is a teacher's pet who wanted to impress me with his extra credit. Joke's on him, because every second Heath held me hostage, the less I liked him.

When I finally managed to kick the kid out, it was well past six in the evening. I thought Sarah was going to be upset with me, but she said she understood and that she was feeling under the weather.

I offered to bring her soup, medicine, and anything else she might need. I longed to take care of her and show her I'm a good Daddy, not just with a strong hand when she needs it, but with a gentle touch as well.

Sarah kept insisting she just needed rest, and while I wanted to bust her door down and force feed her chicken noodle soup, things are still new between us. I made sure to text her throughout the weekend, though I didn't get much of a response. I figured she was resting. It took every goddamn ounce of control not to call her repeatedly until she picked up, but if my princess really wasn't feeling well, sleep is what she needed most.

We agreed to only see each other on weekends, but now I know that was an idiotic idea. I need to see Sarah every fucking day, need her smiles, her laughter, her sparkling teal eyes that remind me there is still good in the world. I thought I was setting a good boundary to try and protect both my job and Sarah's propriety, but the cost is just too much. I don't want texts, I want to hear every word as it falls from her lips.

I plan on telling my little girl just that as soon as I finally see her.

The door to the classroom swings open with a bang as I step inside, swiveling my head back and forth to see if Sarah is here. My shoulders sag when I see the lecture hall is empty. I trudge to the front of the room, setting my satchel down before deflating into the chair.

Something isn't right. I called Sarah yesterday, but it went to voicemail. I figured she was in class and would call me back. She didn't. I sent her a text last night, saying if she didn't answer, I was going to come knocking on her door. I got a simple reply, **I'm okay, just tired.**

Bullshit. As much as I wanted to drive over there and spank her for lying to me, I decided to wait until class today. She can't escape me when we're in here. I'll get a good look at her, make sure she's feeling okay, then ask her to stay after. That's when my little girl will learn her lesson about brushing me off.

I shove down the uncomfortable feeling that's been trying to rear its ugly head these last few days. Maybe Sarah is done with me. Maybe she got what she needed - a thrill ride with her older professor - and decided a further relationship wasn't worth it.

But no, my little girl isn't like that. She's pure, sweet, sassy for sure, but so damn genuine. I just can't picture her using me or tossing me aside. We shared something sacred last weekend when we explored each other's desires and shared our hearts. I just need to remind her of that.

I look up when the door opens, then grunt when I see it's just some preppy freshman with a popped collar. I thought that was out of style these days, but then again, maybe it's not on purpose.

More students file into the lecture hall, talking quietly amongst themselves. By now, everyone knows I don't like interruptions or obnoxious chatter. I glance up every so often to see if Sarah is here yet, but I only see a blur of students who look nothing like my princess. Where the hell is she?

The room grows quiet, and I look up, wondering what caused the silence. There doesn't appear to be a disturbance going on, and I'm thoroughly confused until I realize class started five minutes ago. I always start on time, but today, my head is elsewhere. I guess I've scared my students enough for them to shut themselves up when the time comes.

I clear my throat, surveying the room one more time to make sure I somehow didn't miss Sarah's entrance. I know I didn't, though. I fucking feel her whenever she enters a room. I'm drawn to her, pulled toward her as if by compulsion.

Shuffling the papers on my desk around, I look at my notes, then back up at the mostly full lecture hall. I open my mouth to start the lecture, but instead, I dismiss the class.

"You heard me, we're done for the day. Get out of here before I change my mind."

Bewildered students look around at each other, as if daring someone else to get up first to see if it's somehow a joke. Finally, popped collar guy slides out of his seat and leaves, followed by a few more students. I pack everything up in my satchel and shoo the remaining students out before shutting off the lights. I have somewhere more important to be. My little girl needs a lesson, and she needs it right the fuck now.

No sooner do I get into my car than my phone dings with a notification. "About damn time," I mutter, thinking it's my little girl apologizing for being late to class. Looking at the screen, however, it's a number I don't recognize. My thumb hovers over the screen for a second, and then I open the message, curiosity getting the better of me. What I see has acid churning in my gut and crawling up my throat.

A photo of Sarah and me at the medical museum last weekend pops up. She's facing one of the displays of abnormal tumors, her eyes bright and full of curiosity. I have my arms wrapped around her from behind as I kiss the top of her head. Another text comes in, this one a picture of us kissing rather scandalously in my car in the parking lot outside the museum.

"What the fuck?" I roar, slamming my fist down on the steering wheel. I drop my phone to keep from crushing it. Who the hell took these photos? Sarah is *mine*. Before I can rage too much, a final text pops up.

Let her go and these will never see the light of day. Continue your affair, and you'll both suffer.

It all clicks into place. I'm being blackmailed, and I don't need to guess at who is behind this. Is this why Sarah has been avoiding me? Was she really sick this weekend or was she blackmailed as well?

Jesus, I shouldn't have left her alone for so long. I should have insisted on taking care of her. Fuck. *Fuck!* My mind races with the implications of the text, not only for my career, but for Sarah. What did her father threaten her with? Was he aggressive with her? Did he lay hands on her? I can't even process that right now. He's a dead man. Fucking lowlife user. He thinks he has power, but he's not the only one.

I push my fingers through my hair and try calming the fuck down long enough to deal with this shit. My number one priority is getting to Sarah and making sure she's okay. Still, I can put out a few fires before heading to her place to win her back.

Scrolling through my contacts, I shoot a text to David, my best, most studious grad student, and Harold, an old adjunct professor who used to teach philosophy before Christy took over. I give them only the information necessary, along with a nice incentive in the form of a personal check to get them to jump on this opportunity ASAP.

I only need to wait about thirty seconds before both respond, agreeing to my plan.

With that out of the way, I connect my phone to the bluetooth in my car, then dial Reed's number as I drive out of campus and toward my little girl.

"Dylan," Reed greets. He sounds tired, but not as stressed as the last time we talked. His tone doesn't give anything away, so I'm not sure if he knows about Sarah yet or not. Either way, I'm about to break it to him.

"Reed, we need to talk," I start.

"Yes, I assume that's why you're calling me," he says dryly. "Sorry, I'm just..." He groans, the sound muffled as if he's scrubbing a hand down his face. "I hired a nanny."

"Oh. Well, that's good, right?" I don't really have time to listen to this, but I'll give him a few moments to talk. Maybe then he won't take the news so hard.

"No. It's horrible."

"Are you going to fire her, then?"

"No," he grunts harshly. He sighs again. "She's great with Kayla. The two are thick as thieves. But she can't cook for shit and she leaves everything messier than when she found it. And worse yet, she's... she's... she's *distracting*."

"Ah, I see." And I do. I also have someone in my life who started off as quite the distraction. She's turned into so much more, which reminds me that I need to stay focused.

"It's not like that," Reed says in a rush. "It's just... complicated."

"No judgment here, buddy." Reed grunts again. "Listen, speaking of people we shouldn't be attracted to–"

"I'm not–"

"I'm in love with a student," I blurt out before Reed can lie to me and deny whatever is going on between him and the nanny. Silence rings loud and clear on the other end of the line, though I still hear Reed breathing, so I know he's there.

"Fuck," he finally breathes out.

"Yeah. But it's not a fling. It's not an abuse of power, Reed, I swear."

"I know you, Dylan. I don't think you're abusing your power, but... Jesus, could you have picked a less complicated person to fall in love with?"

"Could you?"

Reed scoffs, but doesn't say anything.

"That's what I thought," I say, turning down the road to Sarah's apartment. "I don't have time to go into details right now, but I'm resigning, effective immediately."

"What the hell–"

"My best grad student, along with a trusted adjunct professor, have already agreed to take over the 101 classes. I will email the necessary parties tomorrow and get a plan started on how to move forward in my absence. You don't have to stress about this, I got it covered," I finish in one breath, needing to get it all out there for my friend.

"You're resigning," he repeats, more thoughtfully this time.

"Yes. And as I've just stated, I took care of the details. So..."

Reed finally lets out a hoarse laugh. "So, you think I should accept your resignation already, is that right?"

"I don't care if you accept it, but I wanted to give you the courtesy since you're my friend and all," I grunt.

Reed chuckles, sounding more like the man I knew before his sister passed away. "There's the Dylan Cole I know. Well, I'd warn you against getting your heart stomped on, but it sounds like you're already on the hook with this woman."

"Damn right I am. And there's nowhere else I'd rather be."

"Good luck, man," Reed says, genuinely. "Promise me you'll update me with more details when you get a chance?"

I agree, then hang up, my hands shaking the closer I get to Sarah's building. Pulling into the lot, I put the car in park and then tip my head back, rolling my shoulders to relieve the tension there. I just quit my job. My tenured job, as a respected professor of philosophy. That should rattle me. Instead, I feel free. It was an obstacle in the way of my happily ever after, so of course, I needed to get it out of the way. Sarah is all that matters, and it's time she knows it.

Chapter Twelve

Sarah

I miss Dylan more than words can say, but I'm doing this for him. I have to stay away. Lying to him about being sick was awful, especially when he was so sweet and wanted to come over to take care of me. I longed for that, for my Daddy to cuddle with me and shower me with the affection I've come to crave.

But I had to. Dylan has loved philosophy since childhood. This is his dream job, to be a tenured professor in charge of important studies and brilliant minds. The thought of him losing all of that for me brings tears to my eyes. Even if he somehow chose me, I know he'd regret it later. Why wouldn't he? Surely the novelty of being with a student will wear off soon, and then where will we be?

My intercom buzzes, the shrill sound breaking up my pity party. I'm not expecting anyone, but then again, my dad likes to barge in on a whim. I look down at my sleep shorts, fuzzy slippers, and ratty old sweatshirt, and groan internally just thinking about what he'll have to say about it. I'll have to inform him that this is the appropriate outfit to wear when you're nursing a broken heart.

"Sarah, I know you're in there."

Oh crap! It's Dylan.

I jump off the couch and take a step toward the intercom, then pause. I shouldn't answer. I need to let him go. I couldn't stand the thought of looking at him in class today, so I skipped. I know I can't skip forever, but I hadn't planned that far ahead yet.

Speaking of class, it's not over for another thirty-five minutes. What is Dylan doing here?

"Please let me in, princess. We need to talk."

I wrap my arms around my waist and stand in front of the intercom, staring at the speaker. Does he know we've been caught? I don't think I can handle him officially breaking up with me. Still, I inch forward, somehow drawn to his voice, even through the crackling intercom.

"I miss you," he says, his voice soft and so damn sad. "I know things are complicated right now, but I'm taking care of everything. I need to see you, baby girl. Please," he adds again.

I lift my hand, brushing my fingers over the speaker as if that will bring me closer to him. God, I'm weak and pathetic, but I buzz him in, then stand back and stare at the elevator, not sure if I'm dreading his presence or craving it. Both, if I'm honest. It's going to hurt like a bitch when he leaves me for good, but apparently, I'm a glutton for punishment.

Wringing my hands together, I'm a nervous, trembling wreck by the time the doors on the elevator slide open. It's been days since I've seen Dylan, and the sight of his broad shoulders, dark hair, and golden-brown eyes has me choking back a sob.

It physically hurts, knowing he'll never be mine. I lift my hand to cover my mouth, trying to muffle my crying.

"Sarah, honey..." Dylan's shoulders drop as his face twists up in worry. He rushes to my side, but I take a few steps back, stumbling over a discarded pair of shoes before catching myself on the kitchen table.

"Stay back," I say with a shaky voice. "I can't... I can't..."

"What happened? Jesus, are those bruises on your arm?" He reaches out for my hand, but I yank it away. His touch might just be my breaking point.

"Sarah," he says sternly, his tone brooking no arguments. "Let me see your arm." I shake my head no, my entire body trembling as Dylan moves closer, cornering me against the table. I watch his eyes turn from brown to a soft amber, his features changing from dominant Daddy to something more tender. Something like love.

He reaches for my hand again, and this time, I let him. He gently lifts my arm, tracing over the fingerprint-sized bruises just above my wrist. They are mostly faded by now, but the outline and hint of a dark shadow still remain.

"He's a dead man." It shouldn't thrill me to hear Dylan threaten my father, but I can't deny feeling safe, protected, and a little turned on. Dammit.

Dylan lifts his eyes, his gaze meeting mine once again. My Daddy engulfs me in a hug, and as much as I want to sink into his embrace and forget about everything, some part of me is still sane enough to know that's impossible.

"Let me go," I whimper pathetically.

"No," comes the one-word response.

I fist his shirt and pull him closer, then spread my palms out and shove him away from me. My breaths saw in and out of my lungs, each one more painful than the last. It feels like I'm breathing through a straw, but I still, I try to wiggle out of his hold.

"Stop fighting me, little girl," he murmurs, making my heart trip all over itself. I'm too far gone to give up now, though.

"I can't," I whisper, feeling myself spiral out of control. I manage to duck under his arms, slipping out of his grip. My thoughts are all knotted up somewhere deep inside, twisting and tangling and suffocating me.

Dylan doesn't let me get very far. He wraps his arms around my waist and pulls me against his solid chest. A shiver rolls down my spine when his lips brush against the shell of my ear.

"Calm down, Sarah. I've got you," he murmurs, his hot breath kissing my sensitive skin. "I said I'd take care of everything. I said we were forever. Do you not believe me? Do you not trust me?"

"What does it matter?" I say with more force than I thought I was capable of at the moment. If he holds me any longer, I'm going to break. I need to push him away. It's for his own good.

Dylan grunts and tightens his hold on me. "It matters a whole hell of a lot, seeing as I love you."

"What?" I try wiggling out of his embrace, and to my surprise, he actually lets me go.

And then he presses his hand in between my shoulder blades and bends me over the kitchen table. I catch myself on my hands, then glare at him over my shoulder. Dylan's eyes are nearly black as he rakes his gaze up and down my body.

My legs tremble, and god, am I wet right now? Dylan looks like he's about to rip me in two with his intensity, and yet all I can think about is how he's going to punish me. I mean, what the hell? I can't want that from him anymore. He's not mine.

Dylan slides his hand up and down my spine slowly, like he's savoring the feeling of me beneath his fingertips. He relaxes me with gentle strokes, his touch so unbelievably tender.

And then he smacks my ass so hard I jolt forward and gasp for air. I'm about to scream for him to stop, when the sting fades and sizzles in my veins, dissolving into liquid pleasure.

Dylan massages the sore spot with one hand and gathers my hair up into a ponytail with his other hand, pulling my head back as he bends over me. I gasp when I feel his teeth scraping across my neck and nipping my ear.

"That's for not talking to me first," he growls.

"I couldn't," I whisper, my throat clogged with tears. "My dad was going to ruin you."

He lands another blow to my other cheek, the tingling sensation rocketing through me with jagged edges and tension.

"The only way I can be ruined is if you leave me."

"That... that can't be true."

"Are you calling me a liar, princess?" When I don't answer, he swats my ass again, making me whimper and press my thighs together.

"I'm not worth it," I blurt out. "You'll hate me for ruining your career. Maybe not right now, but some day, you'll realize you made a huge mistake."

I squeeze my eyes shut, bracing myself for another blow. It doesn't happen. In fact, Dylan steps back, leaving me feeling cold and vulnerable.

I'm about to turn around and beg him to keep going, but Dylan tears my little sleep shorts and panties off, exposing more of me. I should protest. I should yell at him to stop touching me, that we can't do this anymore.

Instead, I spread my legs wider and arch my back, wanting him to see. Wanting him to be proud of me for obeying, however messed up that makes me. A soft moan escapes my lips before I can stop it. Dylan growls and cups my ass, spreading my cheeks apart and cursing under his breath again.

"Not worth it?" he grits out, massaging me roughly. "Not fucking *worth it*? That bullshit stops here, little girl. Thought I made it clear we're permanent. Forever. Did you think I was lying?"

My body takes over, leaving my mind spinning and sputtering as I wiggle my hips. Dylan lands three quick smacks to one cheek and then the other before rubbing the heated skin. His hand slides lower, lower, lower, until he's rubbing my pussy from behind.

"Fuck, princess. You're soaking my fingers. You like when Daddy takes control?"

Oh fuck. Oh *fuck*. I cry out as he circles my clit over and over, gasping for breath as that one word sinks down into my very being. Daddy. I've missed his touch, his both rough and tender.

"Answer me, Sarah."

"I...yes," I whisper. He rewards me by sinking two fingers into my spasming channel, massaging my walls and filling me up. The coil in my belly tightens, tightens, tightens with each thrust until tears sting my eyes and I can't breathe. I need to come so bad it hurts.

Dylan withdraws his hand and I nearly collapse from the ache of being denied. I feel him wipe my juices over my ass, some sick part of me loving how filthy it is. He cracks his palm right over the wet spot, making everything that much more intense.

Again, again, again, he spanks me, each one loosening the knot of tangled emotions that's been suffocating me all week.

"That's it, little love," he murmurs into the shell of my ear, pausing his punishment for the moment to tease my entrance again. "I feel you coming apart for me. Let me have it all. I want your orgasm, your secrets, your goddamn heart and soul. Now give it to me, little girl."

Dylan smacks my raw, throbbing pussy and I come so hard my vision flashes white. I can't see, I can't hear, I can't breathe, I can't do anything but let go and *feel* Dylan's commands course through me and push me deeper into my pleasure.

My arms give out and my entire body trembles as tears drip down my cheeks. I cry and come and gasp for air, unfurling before my beastly professor.

"I've got you," Dylan whispers, gathering me up in his arms. He cradles me against his chest, then lifts me up as he strides through my apartment.

He somehow knows where my bedroom is, and steps inside, sitting on the edge of the bed. I curl up on his lap, naked from the waist down, tears still drying on my cheeks.

"You did so good, princess," he praises. "You needed that, didn't you?" I nod my head and bury my face between his neck and shoulder. "Forever, Sarah. You're mine forever. I don't want to hear you talking bad about yourself anymore. I will *never* regret you. How could I, when you've brought so much joy and meaning to my life?"

I tip my head up, needing to look at him. "But your career..."

"Isn't ruined," he finishes. "I said I took care of it, and you need to learn to trust me. But even if it all blew up in my face, I would walk away from it in a heartbeat, knowing you'd be waiting for me on the other side." I sniffle and Dylan rests his forehead on mine. "I love you," he whispers, pressing a kiss to my temple before tipping his head back down to touch mine.

"I love you so much it hurts," I confess.

"Say it again," he groans, nuzzling into the side of my neck.

"I love you, Daddy."

"Love you so much, little girl," he murmurs, raining kisses down on my cheeks, lips, chin, and everywhere he can reach. I can't help but giggle as his stubble tickles my skin. Dylan closes his eyes and breathes in deep. "Love that sound. Need it in my life every single day."

"I'll see what I can do about that," I tease, the last of my heartache slipping away as his golden eyes twinkle down at me.

"Good. Now, let's see about some other sounds I get get you to make."

"Wha-"

Before I can ask what he means, Dylan has my shirt off and is laying me down on the mattress. His eyes never leave my naked body as he strips down, seemingly desperate to get back to me.

He crawls over my body, littering kisses and love bites over my thighs, torso, and breasts before he claims my lips. I moan into his kiss, unleashing every doubt, every worry, every negative thought I've ever had. I give it all to my Daddy, and he gives me his heart in return.

Spreading my legs wider for him and his massive manhood, I slant my hips in an attempt to get him where we both need him to be. I feel the weight of his dick lay across my pussy, as Dylan slowly starts thrusting his hips, dragging that monster back and forth against my slit.

Dylan growls, then rests his forehead on mine. "I love you, baby girl. You're perfect for me. Promise you'll never doubt me again."

The vulnerability in his voice cracks my heart open, and I blink back tears. "I promise," I whisper. "I love you, Daddy. I'm yours, forever."

"Good girl," he praises right before slamming into me with a roar. God, he's stretching me so wide I think I might actually break in two. The pain and pleasure threaten to overtake me and send me flying into an orgasm far too soon.

Dylan buries his head into the side of my neck, biting and sucking on my sensitive skin while hammering in and out of me with wild abandon. I cling to him as he spears me with his cock, our flesh slapping together, our juices mixing and trickling down my ass, making me clench my pussy around him

"Oh fuck, that's it," he groans. I squeeze my tight channel around him again and moan when I feel his entire body ripple in pleasure. I can't believe *I'm* doing that to him. It's invigorating. Addicting. I want to give him more pleasure.

I dig my heels into his muscular ass and tilt my hips, taking him so fucking deep. He growls as I let out a sharp cry. He's filling me so perfectly, each stroke building me up higher and higher. I can feel every vein and ridge of his glorious cock sliding against the swollen walls of my pussy.

Meeting him thrust for thrust, we tear into each other fucking, biting, clawing until we're both covered in sweat and shaking from pleasure. It's feral, the way he's taking me, owning me, rutting into me over and over like a man possessed. I can't tell where he ends, and I begin.

I'm the first to give up the fight, letting my orgasm flood through my system and overwhelm me. I shake underneath him, the force of my climax rattling me to my very core. I'm expecting him to follow me, but instead, he pulls out and throws my legs over his shoulders before stuffing me full of his cock in one, hard thrust.

I cry out, a jagged, broken sound as he snaps his hips against the back of my thighs and hits the absolute end of me with each powerful stroke. When he reaches down and wiggles his thumb over my clit, I bow my back off the mattress and squeeze my pussy around him. It's so intense, hanging right on the sharp edge of total ecstasy.

"Again," he demands.

My movements become erratic as he breaks me apart with his thick dick. He pinches my clit and I scream as my pussy knots around him again and again. Without any warning, Dylan pulls out of me and flips me on my stomach. I'm still shuddering from my last orgasm as he slides inside of my still-convulsing little hole.

"Jesus Christ, so good. Love being inside you, little girl," he groans.

I whimper and give myself over to him once again. He's completely overpowering me, and I love it. I can't come again, I know it. There's no way that's physically possible, right? And yet...

Dylan spanks me. Hard. Hard enough to leave a mark. Hard enough to make me cry. Hard enough to make me come.

I sob my release, feeling it drip down my thighs in waves and pool on the sheets beneath me.

He fucks me faster, gripping my hair, teasing my breasts. I roll my hips, taking him deeper still. He growls and rips into me, fucking me hard, pulling my hair, slapping my ass. He doesn't hold back. He fucks my throbbing, raw pussy rough and hard.

The pressure builds up immediately and another orgasm splinters into the first one before it is even finished. It's so damn intense, ripping through my body quickly and devastatingly, leaving me weak and panting for air.

"That's right," he growls. "Feel it. Feel it all over your gorgeous fucking body."

I thrash beneath him while he slips an arm under my hips to hold my quivering body up as he slams into me in erratic, jerky thrusts. I can tell he's close, so I use up the very last of my strength to push my ass back into him and squeeze my pussy around that fat fucking cock of his.

"Oh shit, shit, I'm coming, I'm fucking—"

Some primal sound is ripped from the depths of his very being as he empties himself deep inside of me. I feel him twitch and coat my cunt with his sticky, hot cum. He fills me up to the brim, and then fills me up again, his huge load soaking my thighs as he keeps coming and coming.

I can't take anymore. My arms and legs give out and I collapse on the bed. Dylan falls on top of me, catching himself on his forearms at the last minute. He rests his forehead in between my shoulder blades. I feel his hot breath skate across my skin in short bursts as he comes down from that incredible high.

Eventually, Dylan rolls over, taking me with him. Sweat dries on our bodies as he holds me close, trailing his fingers up and down my spine while whispering soothing words against the top of my head.

I must have dozed off, because the next thing I remember is being startled awake by my phone. Panic grips me, thinking it's my father. Dylan squeezes me in a hug and tips my chin up so we're face to face.

"I'm right here," he murmurs. "We'll deal with whoever it is together." I nod my head, not sure how he could read my thoughts, but no longer questioning it.

I grab my phone off the bedside table, sighing with relief when I see Faye's name pop up. "False alarm," I tell Dylan. "It's just my bestie." I answer the phone even though Dylan frowns. It's kind of adorable, like he's not ready to share me with the world. "Hi, Faye," I greet.

"Girl! There you are. I'm worried about you. You went silent on me last week. What's going on?"

"I'm sorry, I know. Will it make you feel better if I told you it's all worked out now?"

She huffs out a breath, though I can tell she's mostly over it. "I guess. But what was *it,* exactly?"

Dylan leans over, peppering a line of kisses over my shoulder and down my back. I turn to look at him, noticing he's already hard, and the lust in his eyes lets me know I need to hang up soon.

"What's going on with you?" I ask, smirking when Dylan grunts in disapproval.

"My mom and her new husband are driving me nuts!" Faye exclaims. I knew she'd take the bait. I have no doubt we'll be talking more about Dylan and me, but for now, Faye takes the hint to change the subject. "And my new stepbrother is... infuriating," she says with an exasperated sigh. "He's seriously the worst. *Jasper.* Ugh." She says his name like a swear word, making me laugh.

"What's his deal?"

Dylan sweeps my hair back, then sucks on my neck, nipping me just below my ear and making me tremble. I rock my hips against his throbbing erection, grinning when I feel him twitch and lengthen against my ass.

"For one, he's an arrogant jerk," Faye starts. "He thinks he knows me just because I come from money."

"Hmm. Sounds familiar," I muse. Dylan bites my shoulder, making me stifle a laugh.

"Jasper seems annoyed by me all the damn time, yet he doesn't want me going out. He got all pissy last night when I said I was going over to Taylor's house. I mean, what the hell?"

"Maybe he thought Taylor was a guy?"

Faye snorts. "Why would that matter?"

I shrug, even though I know she can't see me. I have a feeling Jasper might have a jealous streak in him. One that Faye unknowingly triggered.

I'm about to tell her just that, but apparently, Dylan is done waiting his turn. He grabs my phone out of my hand and gives me a wink.

"Sarah is indisposed at the moment," he growls into the phone. My eyes bug out of my head, but then I hear Faye's bright, boisterous laughter.

"Tell your girl we have A LOT to talk about once she's... dressed."

I roll my eyes.

"I will. I'm sure we'll meet soon, if you're important to my princess."

"Oh my god, *princess?* We have SO MUCH to cover. Tell her–"

"Time's up," Dylan says, hanging up the phone and tossing it aside.

I feign annoyance at him, but Dylan kisses away any and every thought besides the way he's owning me with his mouth.

"Need you," he whispers onto my lips.

"Again?" I tease, as I melt into his touch.

"Always, princess. Forever, remember?"

"Forever."

Epilogue

Dylan

"Did you brush your teeth, Evan?" I ask our six-year-old. He nods his head enthusiastically, but then clamps his mouth shut so I can't inspect his teeth. I raise an eyebrow at him, and he sighs before marching back to the bathroom.

I chuckle, then head to Eleanor's room to check on her. Our sweet four-year-old is all tucked in bed, and Sarah is sitting next to her, reading from her favorite book. My heart aches from all the love I have for my family.

Sarah looks at me over her shoulder, gifting me with a soft smile and bright teal eyes. I'll never get over how stunning she is, and how lucky I am to have her as my wife.

We waited until Sarah graduated from college to get married, though I would have taken her to the courthouse and put a ring on her finger as soon as possible if she had let me. In the end, I agreed that my princess deserved the wedding of her dreams.

"Are you going to join us?" Sarah asks, her eyes twinkling as if she knows what's on my mind.

"Of course. Story time with my two favorite girls? How could I pass that up?"

I crouch down on the floor, next to Sarah, leaning against the bed. Eleanor blows me a kiss, and I catch it before sending her one right back. She's incredibly sweet, just like her mother. She also has a sassy streak. Just like her mother.

Sarah turns the page in Eleanor's favorite book, then holds it with one hand while combing her fingers through my hair with the other. I relax against my woman, letting her tender touch ground me in this moment.

"One day, the princess decided to leave the castle and venture out on her own..." Sarah continues the story, her melodic voice washing over me, settling me down even more.

It's been an incredible seven years with my wife. She got a job working at the trauma ward in a nearby hospital, then transferred to pediatrics a few years ago. She's loved working with children and comforting them when they're at their most vulnerable. There are plenty of hard days, when her patients struggle and occasionally don't make it. I'm here every single time, pouring out my love and support for the woman who has changed everything about me for the better.

Dealing with Sarah's father was easier than I anticipated. The man was a dirty politician through and through, and it didn't take long to find which threads to pull at to make his career unravel completely. After he was ousted and shamed, he scurried away into the shadows to lick his wounds. That's when I paid him a visit and gave him a few more wounds. He thought he could harm my little girl and not pay the consequences? I could have done more damage, but a broken nose and wrist was enough to teach him a lesson.

"The princess didn't *need* a prince to save her, but she found she *wanted* him by her side forever. Thus, the two lived..."

"Happily ever after," I finish for her, tilting my head up to meet her gaze. Eleanor is snoring softly, her cute, round cheeks slightly flushed from sleep.

"Happily ever after," Sarah echos, her smile hitting me square in the chest.

We get up and take turns kissing Eleanor on the head before leaving her room. I place my hands on Sarah's hips, spinning her around so her back is against the hallway wall. Sarah grins up at me, her clear teal eyes so full of love it's hard to catch my breath.

"Did my princess get her happily ever after as well?"

I murmur against the shell of her ear before kissing down her neck.

"She definitely did," Sarah breathes out, melting against the wall and letting me nuzzle against her.

I'm about to drag her back to our room when we hear, "Ew! Ughhhh!"

Sarah giggles as I sigh, then she pushes me away to face our son.

"Did you brush your teeth?" she asks.

"Yesssss," Evan whines. "For real this time." He looks at me, making me laugh with his exasperated tone. Evan opens his mouth for inspection, to which Sarah gives him a nod of approval.

"Off to bed with you then," I say, shooing him to his room. "Mom and I will be right in." Evan scurries off, probably hoping to get all of his toys out before we can get in there and stop him.

"Where were we?" I whisper, drawing Sarah into my arms and rocking her back and forth.

"I think I was telling you how amazing you are, and how happy I am."

I tilt Sarah's head up, then pepper kisses over her forehead, cheeks, nose, and finally, her lips.

"Love you so much, princess," I tell her before kissing her again.

"Love you more." I'm about to protest when she adds, "Daddy."

I groan and give her a peck on the lips before spinning her out of my arms. "You go tuck Evan into bed. I'll be waiting for you in our room."

"Oh yeah?" she says with a sexy little smirk. God, she's somehow more beautiful now than when we first met.

"Yes, little girl. And don't keep me waiting long."

Her smile lights me up, filling my chest with pride and joy, while intensifying my need to claim her over and over. I'll never get enough of her. Good thing she's mine forever.

Connect with me!

Check out my website, cameronhart.net[1], for sneak previews on my latest projects.

Follow me on social media:

Facebook Page - facebook.com/cameronhartauthor
Instagram - instagram.com/cameron.hart.author
TikTok - tiktok.com/@author.cameron.hart
Goodreads - goodreads.com/16081533.Cameron_Hart
Bookbub - bookbub.com/authors/cameron-hart

---

1. https://cameronhart.net/